Becoming
ROSEMARY

"Good books inform, but
great books transform."
– Edgar Dale

The Daniel P. Woolsey Library
of Children's and Adolescent Books

OTHER YEARLING BOOKS YOU WILL ENJOY:

THE WITCH OF BLACKBIRD POND, *Elizabeth George Speare*
THE SIGN OF THE BEAVER, *Elizabeth George Speare*
I AM REGINA, *Sally M. Keehn*
MOON OF TWO DARK HORSES, *Sally M. Keehn*
BESS'S LOG CABIN QUILT, *D. Anne Love*
DAKOTA SPRING, *D. Anne Love*
MY LONE STAR SUMMER, *D. Anne Love*
FAMILY TREE, *Katherine Ayres*
JOHNNY TREMAIN, *Esther Forbes*
THE SLAVE DANCER, *Paula Fox*

YEARLING BOOKS are designed especially to entertain and enlighten young people. Patricia Reilly Giff, consultant to this series, received her bachelor's degree from Marymount College and a master's degree in history from St. John's University. She holds a Professional Diploma in Reading and a Doctorate of Humane Letters from Hofstra University. She was a teacher and reading consultant for many years, and is the author of numerous books for young readers.

Becoming
ROSEMARY

Frances M. Wood

A YEARLING BOOK

Published by
Bantam Doubleday Dell Books for Young Readers
a division of
Bantam Doubleday Dell Publishing Group, Inc.
1540 Broadway
New York, New York 10036

Visit us on the Web! www.bdd.com

Educators and librarians, visit the BDD Teacher's
Resource Center at www.bdd.com/teachers

ISBN: 0-440-41238-2

Reprinted by arrangement with Delacorte Press

Printed in the United States of America

June 1998

10 9 8 7 6 5 4 3 2 1

OPM

For Brian, forever

and for
Kathleen M. Wood, M.D.

CONTENTS

CHAPTER 1

Rosemary

Rosemary *is a watching child.* That is what the Indian told Con during one of their long, absolutely silent conversations. *She has eyes like a damselfly. She looks frontward, backward, sideways.*

Rosemary is twelve years old, Con replied, as if Rosemary's age explained everything.

And Rosemary, sitting on the bank above the river, watching, spying, hoping to hear, looked from her sister on this side of the river to the Indian on the other side. She heard nothing. She didn't see a mouth move.

Rosemary picked up the end of her braid and chewed it. "Ugh," she said, and hers was the only human voice that the river heard that day, unless you counted the almost-voices from behind the waterfall up above the bend. Rose-mary, when she was lonely, did count those voices: murmurs and calls and songs that she could never quite hear, that sounded as if they were at the end of a tunnel, that perhaps came from a promised land far away.

"Ugh," Rosemary said again. She dropped the strawlike taste of her hair and stood. She didn't try to be quiet as she walked away. She liked the crinkle of last autumn's leaves beneath her bare feet. She liked the feel of kid-leather-soft leaf flesh, the bend and snap of leaf bone. Her walk was stately at first, like that of a princess or queen. But then her toes began to curl, and her feet began to skip, and soon she was running up the little path that she shared with rabbits and wild turkeys to the kitchen garden behind her home.

"They're doing it again," she told her mother importantly.

"Mmm," said Althea.

"They don't say *anything*! They just sit and look at each other."

"You don't have to talk to be friends."

"I wish I had a friend," Rosemary said. Her

mood changed abruptly. This was happening to her, now, more and more often. She would feel one way, and then a moment later she would feel something completely different. It was unsettling.

Althea looked up at her youngest daughter. "You have many friends," she said gently.

Rosemary squatted down beside her mother and began pulling lettuce. "I wish," she said, and she sat back on her heels, "that I was rich and smart and beautiful. And then—"

"And then you wouldn't be my Rosemary," said Althea. "You would be just like all the other rich, smart, beautiful girls. You wouldn't be you."

"Sometimes I wouldn't mind," Rosemary said gravely, "not being me."

Althea laughed. "This is the first lettuce," she said, and her voice was full and rich and satisfied, "for the first lettuce salad of the season. We'll have it with cooked eggs and blackberry vinegar. . . ."

But Rosemary was standing up again, her collection of lettuce leaves held loosely in the front of her shift, her hands holding the cloth away from her body, her long, bare, scratched legs visible to her thighs. "I'll take these in," she sighed.

"Tell A-Two to put them in cool water," Althea called after her.

A-Two was the only one of the family inside the house. She was clacking at her loom. She had pushed and shoved and heaved until the loom now stood before the front doorway. The afternoon sun slanted in through the front door, glided over the loom, printed a pattern on the floor at A-Two's back, and then, before it could peter into shadow, joined up with the glare of light that barely intruded through the back doorway.

A-Two, the center of all this sunshine, was muttering under her breath: "Blue, then white. White, then blue." Her feet and hands were nimble and skilled. The cloth, a coverlet for a neighbor who had promised a baby goat in exchange, shone prettily in the light.

"A-Two," said Rosemary.

"Oh, stop it!" said A-Two. "Just stop it!" And she stopped herself, her right hand over her left, her feet teetering on the treadles. "You always tangle me up. Why do you have to talk? Why does anybody have to talk? Do I have to tell everybody this a thousand times? Don't talk!"

"Mama wants you to put the lettuce in cool water," Rosemary said in an injured tone of voice.

"Do it yourself," said A-Two. Her left hand crossed her right, her feet began to work, and she returned to the mathematical intricacies of her loom.

Rosemary sighed. She walked around A-Two to the table, put her finger into a jug of water, considered, and decided that the water was cool enough. She took down a flat china bowl from the cupboard and dumped in the lettuce. She looked back at A-Two.

Sometimes Rosemary couldn't decide which of her two sisters she liked better, or liked less. A-Two was certainly the prettier, there was no disputing that fact. Con was taller than their father: She had wider shoulders and bigger feet. A-Two was just tall enough to look slender, just small enough to appear dainty, and just graceful enough to seem sweet.

But unlike Con, A-Two was often crotchety. Rosemary left her second sister and wandered out onto the porch, then down to the hard-packed earth, where a few chickens were anticipating supper. "Not yet, Chloe. Not yet." Rosemary knew all the chickens by name; they were her special charge.

She raised her arms above her head, stretched, yawned, and looked to see what she could see: the garden where her mother still worked, the woodshed, the chicken house, the barn; beyond that, the field where her father plowed the earth with the family's one ox; surrounding it all, the forest, the wonderful, wonderful forest. The forest, where right now the mountain laurel was coming into bloom, and the Solomon's seal, and the coral honeysuckle, and the sundrops, and the green-and-purple jack-in-the-pulpits. Where Rosemary stood, the sun was a hot helmet upon her head; but in the forest, the sun would be far, far away.

That's what she would do, she decided. She would return to the forest. She headed around the far side of the house, away from the kitchen

6

garden. She saw Thomas Small coming up the wagon path. "Hello, Thomas," she said.

"Rosie," he answered.

Rosemary skipped forward to meet him. Thomas carried a length of rope in his arms, rope that Rosemary remembered as having been borrowed from her father. Thomas glanced toward the front door. A-Two's loom still clacked with a beat as perfect and regular as a song's. Beneath that beat—Rosemary listened very carefully—A-Two's voice rose and fell like water.

"I wouldn't disturb her," Rosemary warned Thomas. "I wouldn't go *near* her today."

Thomas continued walking toward the front door.

"She's not nice at all," said Rosemary, "and if you disturb her, she'll hate you."

Thomas frowned.

"Of course, she doesn't like you very much anyway," Rosemary remarked thoughtfully.

Thomas flushed. His steps faltered, halted. He turned sharply right and marched toward the barn. Rosemary lingered around the wagon path until he came out of the barn without the rope. Without another glance at her or the front door, he marched back home.

"Well!" Rosemary said softly to herself. She walked between field and pasture, waved to her father when he looked her way, and then, when he wasn't looking, folded herself into the forest like cream being stirred into a pudding.

The sun stopped, the heat stopped. She was standing at the bottom of a great green depth, inhaling the moist and slightly bitter breath of leaves. The air was as thick as water, the light was milky and pale. Rosemary raised her arms and, as if she were swimming, followed a path-less trail to a spy tree from which she could again see Con and the Indian.

They sat as before, exactly as before. The Indian—on his side of the river—sat cross-legged but straight-backed, a hand on each knee. He wore a loincloth and a farmer's hat. Con— twenty stepping-stones across from him—rested with her back against a tree.

Rosemary eyed the stepping-stones. She wouldn't have been surprised to see a rock, even a boulder, suddenly rise up and turn end over end, splashing water like a fish. Rocks sometimes did that when Con was around. But today the rocks lay still; Con wasn't in a playful mood. She was resting. She wasn't, Rosemary observed righteously, doing any kind of work at all.

Rosemary, being a good worker and a producing member of the family, went to look for ginseng. She walked carefully this time, with her head down, looking for three leaves, five leaflets, and a cluster of green-white flowers. She walked where the oak and hickory leaves— hundreds of years deep on the forest floor— were crushed down to a loam that was as dark as coffee. There she found her leaflets and her flowers. With a pointed stick, she began to dig.

At first she dug determinedly. Then she dug with pleasure. She liked the crumble of the earth in her hands, its rich, rich smell. It was a smell that made her think of Christmas cakes and home, of her mother's kiss and her father's smile. The earth was all the pleasures of the familiar. The ginseng root, when she found it, was wealth, foreign lands, excitement.

Whenever Rosemary gathered a basket of

ginseng, her father took it to the mill. The miller sold it to one of the traveling merchants who came down the road from the courthouse town, many miles away. The merchant carried the ginseng for hundreds of miles until he reached the ocean. Then the ginseng traveled for thousands of miles on a ship, until it was sold in a country where the people were actually yellow.

Yellow people. Not pink or pale brown, like most of the people Rosemary knew. Not black-brown, like the squire's Seth, or reddish brown, like the Indian. But yellow. The yellow of a black-eyed Susan, of a buttercup, of a sundrop at the field's edge. The sundrop was the prettiest yellow, almost the color of the sun itself when the sky was especially blue. That was the yellow that Rosemary chose for those wonderful, distant people. Sundrop yellow skin, and black, black hair. Nobody had ever told Rosemary what color their eyes might be, so in most of her musings she painted them green. Bright green. She was digging ginseng for magical people with eyes the color of grass in sunlight.

The root, when she finally had it out of the

ground, was as long as her forearm and as wizened as a newborn baby's face. Rosemary hefted it and, with old experience, guessed that it weighed about half a pound. Proud of herself, she ran down to the river, where she washed her hands. With peaceful satisfaction she bunched up her shift and waded along the river's edge, looking for a rock large enough to sit on.

"Ah!" she breathed, and for a long while she stood in the water, not moving.

Before her, on a wide, flat rock, a dozen young butterflies pulsed their wings: open, closed, open, closed, open, closed. From where she stood, Rosemary could see the sticky film on those wings. Even as she watched, the stickiness dried, and one butterfly, and then another, took flight. They flew like titmouse chicks new from the nest, traveling up with the breeze, down with the wind, their paths determined by the air around them, not by their skill.

"Ah!" Rosemary sighed again, and she was happy. All the butterflies were in the air now, as yellow as autumn leaves. Now they would learn to fly; now they could take care of themselves. With their wings spread and dried, their danger time was past. Not one was starting adult life with glued wings, a cripple.

"Ro-sie!"

The call was faint but clear. It was her mother, Althea, calling. Rosemary pounded out of the river, letting her shift fall back into place as she ran. When she reached her front door she stopped, smoothed down the hair around her face, and stepped daintily across the threshold.

A-Two's loom was gathering evening shadows. A-Two herself was setting the table with assorted plates and mugs and spoons. Rosemary's lettuce, drained of its water, sat in the middle of the table with crumbled hard-cooked eggs scattered over the leaves. Althea was sliding corn bread onto a wooden board. Con sliced away at a heavily salted ham. Colin, the father of the family, his beard still damp from a wash outside, stepped in through the back doorway and smiled a special smile at Rosemary.

"Let us sit," he said. And when all of his family were seated, Colin began to pray: "O Lord, I give you thanks for this meal and for the health of my good wife, myself, my daughters Constance, Althea the Second, and Rosemary, and for all of the pleasures and joys of this day in the year of our Lord 1790."

Early evening was always a time of chores. After supper Rosemary tended to her chickens. She carried a basket of corn into the back yard, tossed the kernels onto the ground, closed her eyes, and listened. She could almost always tell—by cackle, by grumble—which hen was coming home from the forest. Chloe, then Persephone, Jezebel, Portia. There was a lull in the hen talk, a mighty *karoo!* Rosemary opened her eyes. The rooster, Zeus, had arrived. He stood guard over corn and harem. With nothing but the power of his presence, he kept the hens waiting at the very edge of the scattering of corn. The last straggler—Rachel—arrived. Zeus stepped through his wives and pecked up a kernel. The hens lunged.

They pecked, they quarreled, they stepped on each other's toes. When all the corn was gone, Rosemary heaved Zeus up into her arms. "Bedtime," she announced. With Zeus as proudly balanced as a cat, she led the hens into the henhouse.

This was a special time of day for Rosemary. She almost always sat with her chicken friends while they settled for the night. Sometimes she talked to them. Sometimes she sang. Sometimes she closed her eyes and tried to imagine what they might dream, but all she could see behind her eyelids were specks of corn and forest bugs and the soft, green shoots of spring. She could see all that just as well with her eyes open.

"Would you like to hear the story of your name, Chloe?" she offered. But before she could begin, heavy feet came pounding down the wagon path. Within two seconds Rosemary was out of the chicken house, the door latched. She raced Thomas Small for the big house.

Thomas ran in through the front doorway. Rosemary skidded in through the back. Her mother and sisters turned from their tasks at the table and fireplace. Thomas bumped into A-Two's loom. Rosemary's father took his pipe from his mouth. "Thomas?" he said.

"Pa sent me." Thomas was breathing so hard

that his words had no edges; they sounded like the wind. "It's Bella. Calving. Trouble."

"Ease up, boy. Tell me. What trouble?"

"Calf won't come. Can't reach it. Bella's bleeding, buckets!"

"Oh, no!" said Althea.

Colin put down his pipe.

"Take this," said Althea, "and this." She grabbed herbs from the cupboard, from where they hung below the ceiling, and from where they were nailed beside the chimney.

"Thank you, ma'am," said Thomas.

"Break them in your hands," Althea directed Colin. "Rub them into a powder. Put it into the cow, as far as you can reach. It will help the calf to come forth."

Colin and Thomas, avoiding the loom, rushed out the back door.

Althea, A-Two, and Rosemary all looked at Con. Con shook her head. "I'm trying, but I can't hear her heartbeat. I think Bella is dead."

Althea sighed. A-Two returned to banking the fire. Rosemary lingered by the table. "Thomas didn't look at you," she said to A-Two.

15

"Thomas doesn't always look at me."

"Almost always." Rosemary was pert.

"Can't you keep her quiet, Mama?"

"Thomas is a fine young man," Althea said absently.

"Fine?" A-Two exclaimed. "How can a man be fine if he doesn't wear shoes?"

Rosemary looked down at her own bare feet, and then at A-Two's. Rosemary's feet were actually cleaner.

"The Smalls are no wealthier than we are," said Althea. "They can't afford to wear shoes on every occasion."

"How can a man be fine," A-Two argued, "if he isn't rich?"

"That's foolishness speaking!" Althea was sharp.

A-Two's petulance collapsed like a punctured pig's bladder. "He isn't special," she muttered.

"Thomas is the son of your father's oldest friend." Althea's voice ended the conversation.

It was late now, late enough for bed. Rosemary went up the ladder-stairs to the big attic room that she shared with her sisters. She lay down on her pallet and tried to see stars

16

through the chinks in the roof. Then she sat up and pulled her box out of the wall. Sometimes the box was a place for treasures, but more often it was just a plug for a gap between two logs. Rosemary peered through the gap. She saw the sky, she saw stars, she saw Con walking back from the barn after checking on their own milk cow and the ox. Rosemary put the box back into its place. She went to sleep.

When she awakened, the attic room was completely black. No moonlight or starlight came through any chink or gap. Rosemary wondered, briefly, what it was that had caused her to wake up. Her sisters were silent, motionless. Sleepily Rosemary turned her head so that her ear moved closer to the plank floor. She closed her eyes again. She thought she heard someone quietly grieving far below, but only her parents slept at ground level.

"You're tired." It was her mother speaking, from the big bed beside A-Two's loom. Rosemary opened her eyes. "You feel it so because you're tired."

"Oh, Allie!" That was Rosemary's father.

"They'll take the meat from the cow."

17

"They've lost her milk forever."

"There will be other milk cows."

"You didn't see it, Allie! All twisted and tangled inside its mother; her innards ripped. It was a monster, a godless monster! A monster calf!"

"Did it live?"

"How could it? With two heads!"

Rosemary's eyes opened even wider.

"It tore apart its mother. It *killed* its mother, and then it died just as we pulled it loose."

"I could have helped," Althea mused.

"Never!" There was panic in Colin's voice.

"There are things that I could do. Could have done. No one would have known."

"No, Althea. Not that. Never. We'll help in the ordinary ways: with butter, with cheese, with friendship." Colin had control of his voice now; he was firm.

The conversation continued, but along familiar lines: Colin hoped to finish his plowing the next day, Althea asked about the haying. Rosemary drifted back to sleep.

She dreamt: not about two-headed calves, but about the rooster, Zeus. Zeus, standing on top of the woodshed, throwing hammers onto the ground, each hammer hitting the ground with a rumble, a roar, a Colin-like snore. The rumbles became louder, almost majestic; with each hammer, Zeus released a blaze of light.

This time Rosemary was wide awake when she opened her eyes. She sat up and pulled her box from the wall. She saw the woodshed, without a rooster, momentarily lit from behind. Then she heard real thunder that easily drowned out her father's noisy sleep. Rosemary gasped as a ball of fire moved down a tree at the edge of the forest.

The back door opened, and somebody stepped out onto the porch. Rosemary had to wait a moment to see that the somebody was her mother. Althea went to stand in the yard.

The next clap, the next flash, happened together. The sound was as big as the farmstead. The flash aimed straight at the barn. Althea's hand moved upward, as fast as fire. The lightning, in midjourney, stopped; it doubled back on itself, shooting skyward, making an eerie hairpin of light.

Althea pushed against the air with both

hands. The next flash of lightning was over the river. The next clap of thunder was smaller, trailing the flash by a moment. The rain came, and Althea returned inside.

Rosemary settled back upon her pallet. She could still hear her father's snores as background to the rainfall. Her sisters still slept. Rosemary felt very safe, very safe indeed. She turned onto her side and she, too, slept the rest of the night away.

CHAPTER 2

The Mill

Rosemary sat at the very back of the wagon, her legs dangling over the open edge, her petticoat spread out carefully beneath her as a barrier against the splinters. She could have sat up front with her father, where the wagon seat was well planed and almost splinter-free, but she preferred to take her chances at the back. She enjoyed the special feeling that went along with leaving the countryside, as opposed to what a person felt upon arriving. Every flower or shrub or tree that Colin greeted, Rosemary said goodbye to. It was a sweet feeling, but also sad.

The wagon bed, behind Rosemary, was filled with poles: long, strong, supple poles that had been hickory saplings growing in swampy spots beside the river. Rosemary and Con had helped to cut them; Colin had soaked them in the river overnight. Now he was taking them to the mill. The miller's son would take the poles even farther up the river, to the courthouse town, where he would sell them to the barrel-maker.

" 'The Lord protects us here below,' " sang Colin. " 'Our minds, our hearts He will always know . . .' "

Rosemary bounced happily. " 'Let us then our love increase,' " she joined in. " 'Spite and anger thus to cease.' " She had her own reason to be contented: Somewhere at the head of the wagon bed, tucked beneath the poles, was a basket full of ginseng roots. The sundrop people believed that ginseng would keep them young forever. Rosemary, who feared that she would never be anything but young, had plans. With her ginseng money she intended to buy sugar, brown sugar.

The ox plodded onward. When it finally stopped, Rosemary hopped down from the wagon. While Colin unloaded the poles, she chased down to the millpond, inspected the water for fish, and then dashed back to the wagon. She picked up her basket of ginseng, brushed off the front of her petticoat, and—with sedate steps—preceded her father into the mill. "Good morning, miller," she said, as gracious as any lady come to call.

"Why, good morning, miss," the miller responded with equal graciousness. He winked at Colin. "And what might I do for you today?"

Rosemary held up her ginseng basket, and the miller stepped away from his machinery. Rosemary inspected his feet: Underneath a thick coating of flour (white on top, black beneath), his feet were indisputably bare. She raised her nose higher. "I expect a good price, now," she said.

"But of course," the miller agreed.

Rosemary put her basket down on the counter that was reserved for such transactions and, bare feet and high society forgotten, waited eagerly for the miller's verdict.

"Um," said the miller. "Uh-huh." He took root after root from the basket, inspecting each one. When he got to the big root, the root half as long as Rosemary's arm, he paused. "A big one," he said. "Very big. But dug too soon."

"No!" said Rosemary.

"It's going to shrink," said the miller. "You know that, Rosie."

Rosemary sighed.

"But," said the miller, "a good price overall. How do you want your pay?"

"In sugar, of course." Rosemary turned to see if her father was watching. But Colin was over by the stove, where bags of grain and flour were piled to make chairs and benches, and where even now—on such a fine day—six men were gathered. "Brown sugar."

"Brown sugar for the family," the miller agreed. "And for you—perhaps, maybe—a chip of white sugar." Rosemary turned again. The miller was holding out a pin and a length of horsehair. "Go on, Rosie. Catch a fish!"

It was the miller's special treat: He allowed all the local children to fish in his pond—as long as they sold their fish right back to him. In exchange for each fish, the miller gave away a chip of white sugar, absolutely pure and absolutely sweet, the kind of sugar that only the wealthiest man in the neighborhood, Squire Chalmers, could afford to buy.

Rosemary took her tackle outside. No other children were fishing at the pond this day. Only Black Seth, Squire Chalmers's man—the only slave Rosemary had ever seen—sat there in the sun. Rosemary eyed Seth, stared at her horsehair line, and then eyed him again. This time he caught her. He smiled: white, white teeth against a black-brown face. "What are you doing here today, Seth?" she asked.

"The mistress needs flour," he answered.

"Baking day tomorrow?"

"Baking days all next week. The squire's son is coming home."

"The squire has a son?"

"By his first wife. The boy lives with his mother's family in Williamsburg."

Rosemary absorbed this news. "Is that what they're talking about in there?" she asked, and she nodded toward the mill.

"No. They're talking about Mr. George Washington and the government. And the War of Revolution. I think your papa was a soldier."

"Yes."

25

"Of course, you were just a baby then."

"Did Indians live here when I was a baby? Tribes of them?"

"No. The Indians moved away from this river even before your grandpapa was born, after the first farmers came. There's only the odd one hereabouts. Now and then."

"Oh," said Rosemary, and the conversation died away. Rosemary leaned back so that she was resting on her forearms, her horsehair line wrapped around her wrist, her feet and pin-hook dangling in the water. As lazily as a lizard on a log, she looked around. Back in the trees, she could see the top of the miller's house, with what looked to be a cold chimney. Upstream of the mill, where a healthy brook met the river, two thin plumes of smoke rose into the air: one, Rosemary calculated, from the blacksmith's forge; the other from a fire behind a house. It was almost warm enough to begin cooking out-side.

She swung her eyes away from the river and in an arc up to the wooded ridge. There— almost at the top—was the sharp brown angle of the schoolhouse roof. Rosemary had attended school there two winters ago.

She closed her eyes and remembered: the narrow room with log benches; the teacher stepping in from the lean-to that attached to the back of the schoolhouse; the dozen or so students craning their necks, trying to see into the teacher's private room; the teacher looking directly at each child until that child stopped wriggling and sat still and straight. And then the teacher's voice: "Are you too large to sit?"

The teacher was talking to Con, who stood beside the doorway. Con, who rarely came to the mill, who rarely talked to people outside her own family. Sixteen years old then, Con's head was already higher than the lintel. Con didn't answer the teacher right away; she had just knocked her head, coming in. But the teacher didn't know that. "Are you stupid?" the teacher demanded. "Sit, I said. Sit!" She waved her hand. "Go sit with the babies."

"I've seen girls like her before," the teacher told the miller when he stopped by later for an inspection and a visit. "Excessively large and overdeveloped. It's a problem with what they call the pituitary. Too much phlegm in the child's system. All of her growth has gone into her body, none of it into her brain. An almost adult child, but with the mental abilities of a slug. It happens."

The miller nodded wisely, impressed by the teacher's long and learned words. "Always something different about that girl," he agreed.

"A sad burden for the family, but nothing that science can do. We must be kind and Christian."

The following spring, the teacher left, and school permanently ended. Con had never returned after the first day. But from that day on, everybody in the neighborhood was kind and Christian to her. After years of wondering, they finally felt they understood what it was about Con that made them so uncomfortable when they were around her, what it was that made her so very different: Con suffered from too much phlegm.

And all the while, everybody in Rosemary's

family knew that Con was the best book reader for miles around.

"Wake up, Rosie."

Rosemary grumbled. Someone was touching her shoulder. Her wrist hurt horribly.

"You have a fish."

She opened her eyes and then sat up with a jerk. With Seth's help, Rosemary pulled the fish up onto the dirt. "Do you think it's a two-chipper?" she asked hopefully.

Seth shook his head. "Not even a one-and-a-half."

"Oh, well." Holding the fish by the line, Rosemary took it into the mill. The miller was not—as she had hoped—behind his counter. Instead, he sat with the other men in his parlor of grain sacks. Rosemary went to stand at his shoulder, her fish wriggling and dripping pond water.

"Agricultural reform." Rosemary's father was speaking. "Mr. Washington is an adherent, and so is Thomas Jefferson."

"Book farming!" one of the men hooted.

29

"Crop rotation is an important part of the new methods," Colin continued, ignoring his friend. "The first year, you plant your corn with potatoes—"

"And you grow books!"

"The second year you grow buckwheat, and then you plow it right back in—"

"Buried books!"

"What do you want, Rosie?" asked the miller.

Rosemary held her fish so that it dripped water onto his sleeve.

"Ah!" he said. "A chip!" And with Rosemary's gratitude, he went back to his counter. Rosemary dropped her fish into the bucket at the counter's end and waited. The miller reached to a shelf, took down a cone of hard, white sugar, and with a nail and a little hammer struck off a chip the size of a baby acorn. "For you, miss," he said with a bow. "For a lady as rich as the squire!"

Rosemary smiled politely, allowing the miller his joke.

Sometimes it was best to bite into the chip of sugar, letting it dissolve in one sweet rush. Sometimes it was best to let the little nugget sit under the tongue, slowly melting. Today Rosemary chose the latter method. She followed the miller back to the men's club and settled with a sigh on a corn sack beside her father. Absently Colin patted her hand: ". . . you plant clover your sixth year," he told his neighbors. "And then you're at the top of the cycle: time to plant corn again. The idea is not to wear out the soil. It's called soil conservation."

"Another of your notions, Mr. Weston." A farmer from up the river shook his head at Colin. "Like spring wheat. I hear that you, Mr. Small, and the squire have agreed to experiment with spring wheat. I'll be interested to know how *that* experiment turns out."

Rosemary nudged her father's arm.

"What is it, Rosie?"

Rosemary looked, all the men looked, and the miller rose to his feet. "Ah!" he said. "Welcome! Come in."

A man and a woman—both very handsome, both very black-haired, both very young—stood just inside the doorway. They held hands, which made them look even younger. But the lady's belly pushed out over her feet, and the

31

man's smile was that of an adult. The neighborhood men glanced at, and then looked away from, the lady's belly. Rosemary studied the protuberance with professional curiosity.

"The DiAngelis," the miller announced. "They're the surprise that I've been promising you men!"

"How do you do, ma'am?" the group of men murmured politely.

"Come in," said the miller. "Come in!" And the DiAngelis moved a few steps closer to the grain sacks. "Tell them your trade, Mr. DiAngeli."

"I'm a cooper," said the young man.

"A cooper!" said Colin.

"I was working with my pa down in Wilmington, but when I got married"—Mr. DiAngeli looked at his wife—"I thought I'd set up my own business."

"And us with the nearest barrel-maker ten miles away," said the miller. "So when I heard that a young man was looking for a place to set up his trade, I sent word that we were a place that needed a man just like him. He does good work, too. That barrel you're sitting on, Mr. Henshaw, is one of his."

Like bees to honey, the men buzzed around the barrel, inspecting it up and down. "Looks good," said one.

"Looks fine!" said Colin.

"I told them that they could stay up at the old schoolhouse," said the miller, "until they build their own place or until we find a teacher."

"No need to hurry in your building," said a man. "We haven't had a teacher these last two years."

"And that load of poles you brought in today, Mr. Weston?" the miller continued. "I thought you might just want to sell them to the cooper yourself."

While the men fussed around the barrel and the barrel-maker, Rosemary kept an eye on Mrs. DiAngeli. When she thought that the lady had remained standing long enough, she poked the miller. It took a moment before he understood her message. Then: "Sit down, ma'am," he said; and, as the lady began to lower herself onto a pile of sacks, "unless you'd like to meet the other ladies?"

"I'd like that," said Mrs. DiAngeli. Her voice was soft and musical.

"Rosie . . . ," the miller began, but Rosemary was already at the new lady's side.

"I'll show you, ma'am," she said.

"Take the fish, Rosie," the miller directed.

The bucket was heavy with all the day's fish, which was one reason why Rosemary walked slowly. But mostly, she took her time because the lady was tired. Mrs. DiAngeli didn't mention her weariness, but Rosemary could tell. When they got outside, out where a big wagon stood in the very middle of the wagon path, Rosemary stopped for a look. Mostly what she saw were barrels, but here and there was a chair or a bedstead.

Rosemary continued onward. She followed the little trail that went from the miller's house to the blacksmith's house, taking her fish and lady toward the forge and the fire. She saw the smith working in his open shed, but she didn't wave; he wasn't a sociable man. Instead, she continued right up to the house, set her bucket on the front porch, and led her lady through the house and out again to the back porch. Everybody was in the back yard, just as she had expected: all of the miller's family, all of the smith's family.

The miller's wife was directing the day's activity, which seemed to be soap-making. There was a big kettle in the middle of the yard with an egg floating in it—had to be lye. The smith's oldest boys, Benjie and Frankie, were adding wood to the fire under the kettle. The miller's old-maid daughter, Miss Nancy Proctor, was sniffing at the fat in the scrap bucket. Mrs. Bathsheba, the smith's wife, sat on a stool nursing her youngest, and tenth, child.

It was the miller's daughter-in-law, a baby on her own hip, who first noticed Rosemary. "Rosie?" said Mrs. Olivia Proctor. "Who is that behind you?" For Mrs. DiAngeli still stood within the back doorway, almost covered with shadows.

"A new lady," said Rosemary, and she jumped from the porch into the yard, forcing

Mrs. DiAngeli to step forward, into the sunlight.

"Why, how do you do?" said the ladies. All of them, except for Mrs. Bathsheba, wiped their hands on their aprons and drew near.

In the sunlight, Mrs. DiAngeli's face was white and red: white with exhaustion, red with shyness. "How do you do?" she answered.

"Good heavens!" said the miller's wife. "Benjie!" Her summons was as loud as a call to arms. "Bring a chair."

Benjie stuck his tongue out at Rosemary, Rosemary stuck hers out in turn, and Benjie brought a chair from the house and placed it on the porch.

"Now, sit!" the miller's wife ordered. "You must be the cooper's wife."

Mrs. DiAngeli sat. "My husband's back at the mill," she said. "We just arrived."

"Like this? You traveled like this?" The miller's wife didn't look at or mention Mrs. DiAngeli's belly, but Rosemary knew what she was talking about.

"We traveled slowly, stopping often. We didn't have to come far today."

36

"I had no idea," the miller's wife muttered. "Men!"

"I expect," called Mrs. Bathsheba, from where she still sat, "that you'll want supper?"

Mrs. DiAngeli looked anxiously grateful. "If you don't mind . . ."

"Of course you'll have supper," said the miller's wife. "There's no time today for you to set up housekeeping. We'll all have supper here tonight. Rosemary!" Rosemary appeared at her elbow. "Tell my husband that we'll want the fish down here."

"They're on the front porch," said Rosemary.

"Good. Well, let's get on with this soap-making, and then we'll start thinking about supper. Benjie! Frankie! More wood!" The miller's wife returned to the kettle.

"Mother forgot to introduce herself," the miller's daughter-in-law said, and she sat down on the edge of the porch, putting her own baby to her breast. "We're the Proctor family and the Bathsheba family. The Proctors at the mill, the Bathshebas at the forge. You'll get us all straightened out in time. My Christian name is Olivia."

"Maria DiAngeli," said Mrs. DiAngeli.

"Is that a French name?" called Mrs. Bathsheba, for she sat close enough to hear.

"It's Italian," Mrs. DiAngeli answered.

"Papist, though, I think."

Mrs. DiAngeli blushed even redder.

"But Christian, still," said Mrs. Olivia Proctor.

"I hear the papists spawn devils, not babes," said Mrs. Bathsheba.

Mrs. DiAngeli looked ill.

"Silly lies and superstition," Mrs. Olivia Proctor said shortly. There was a moment of awkward silence, and then Mrs. Olivia Proctor said diffidently, "I didn't like to mention, but I know you'll want to know. . . ."

"Yes," said Mrs. DiAngeli. "Please." Her hands protectively cupped her belly.

"We have a fine midwife. The best, I think, in the region."

"The best in the state," Mrs. Bathsheba corrected. "A God-fearing woman."

"She's never lost a baby, to my knowledge. And she's never lost a mother—"

"Which is more," said Mrs. Bathsheba, "than any papist midwife can claim."

Mrs. Olivia Proctor ignored the interruption. "And if you have a fever or a burn, or if your husband breaks a bone—why, she's a wonder!"

"Once, Mr. Clem Henshaw," said Mrs. Bathsheba, "didn't want to be seen by a woman, so he went all the way up to Hillsborough, to a doctor. And got bled something awful. Came back so weak and pale! Mrs. Weston set him right. Now Mr. Henshaw won't go near a doctor."

"There's something almost magical in her touch," Mrs. Olivia Proctor assured the newcomer.

"Not magic, never magic!" snapped Mrs. Bathsheba. "I tell you, Althea Weston's a God-fearing woman! Nothing sinful in *her* touch."

"When you're settled," said Mrs. Olivia Proctor, "I'll take you to the Weston farmstead. Rosemary here is Mrs. Weston's youngest."

"I met Mr. Weston," said Mrs. DiAngeli. "He brought some poles down to the mill—just today!"

"You and your husband are welcome here," Mrs. Olivia Proctor said warmly. "My father-in-law has often said that with just a few more skilled families, we could become a town!"

The conversation turned to practical matters: farmlands, the schoolhouse roof. Rosemary drifted away from the porch, going the long way around the yard in order not to walk in front of Mrs. Bathsheba. She arrived at the kettle at the same time as Benjie, who was carrying another load of wood. "Look at you!" he said. "Look at your ugly face!"

"You have snot hanging out of your nose," Rosemary returned, and she went to stand beside Miss Nancy Proctor, whom nobody wanted to marry, but who made the best soap around. Miss Nancy Proctor was a thin lady, mostly made of bones. Her elbows, her shoulder blades, her knees—whatever she was wearing, her bones still stuck out. While the miller's wife dispatched and ordered, Miss Nancy Proctor stood in a mystical silence before the kettle, stirring. Rosemary tried to look into the kettle, but the smoke and the lye made her eyes sting.

"Ro-sie!"

Rosemary's head lifted like a deer's.

"That's your papa," said the miller's wife. "Run along."

Rosemary ran as fast as she could, around the house, up the path, to the mill. The cooper's horse and wagon and barrels were gone from the wagon path. Colin's ox and wagon stood on the path instead, pointed toward home. Colin was already seated, looking backward, waiting. When he saw Rosemary, he grinned. Rosemary climbed up beside him. "A big day!" he said.

"A big day," she agreed.

As the ox picked up its feet and plodded onward, she thought of all the things she could tell her mother: about Mrs. DiAngeli, about Mr. DiAngeli, about the chip of sugar. That made her remember. She turned to look. In the wagon bed, assorted packages had been placed inside a brand-new water barrel. "Did we get sugar?" Rosemary asked. "Brown sugar, like Mama said?"

"Coffee, tea, salt," Colin listed. He waited just long enough to tease, and then he added, "Brown sugar."

"Bought with my ginseng?"

"Bought with your ginseng, Miss Rose. A *big* bag of sugar!"

Satisfied, Rosemary settled herself to be comfortable. This time she watched the landscape approach. This time the whole world was coming toward her, opening its arms, welcoming her with what she knew, bidding her—with trees and shrubs and flowers—to come home.

"Do you know, Papa," she said, "I looked at everybody's feet today. And nobody—not even Mrs. DiAngeli—was wearing shoes."

CHAPTER 3

The Squire's

The first light of June, the misty paleness of morning. The cardinal and the wood thrush sang with piercing pureness. Rosemary opened her eyes to slivers of light pushing their way through tiny gaps in the roof and walls. To her half-awakened mind, the birdsong was as rich as summer fruit: a sweet, melting fullness kept taut within the skin of each note. She wriggled her toes and then her feet; then she turned her head. A-Two still slept, but Con's pallet was empty. Rosemary opened her ears to the sounds below. Her mother's wooden spoon bumped against the side of a kettle; Althea was making mush. Colin's feet were conspicuously silent; he was already gone.

Rosemary sat up to take her box from the

wall. Three or four chickens pecked in the yard; Con had already let them out. Rosemary returned the box and lay down again. If A-Two could sleep late, then so could she.

She slept until she felt a toe prodding her ribs. "Lazy!" said A-Two disgustedly. Rosemary didn't bother to answer.

Downstairs there were two bowls of cold mush on the table, and a small pitcher of milk. Rosemary poured milk into her bowl and went outside. She saw her mother in the garden, her father way off in the fields, and Con nowhere. Rosemary sat on the front stoop with her bowl on her knees and watched the day progress.

The sun already warmed the top of the forest. The dew was almost dry. The calls of the morning birds gave way to those of the day birds— the rusty creak of the jay, the rude squawk of the crow. The day moved with all the slowness of the river above a dam. And then Thomas Small came walking down the wagon path.

Rosemary was instantly alert. She finished her mush with a gulp and waited. This time Thomas was carrying a milk bucket, obviously empty. He approached the house like someone invited, hardly noticing Rosemary's presence. "Hello, Thomas," she said when he stepped over her.

"Rosie," he answered.

Rosemary spun around to look inside. A-Two sat slumped at the table. Her hair, barely caught in its nighttime braid, surrounded her head like a bush. Her shift gaped open over her chest, her petticoat was unfastened at the waist, and her feet—Rosemary was glad to see—were absolutely bare.

Thomas stopped, as suddenly as if he had hit a wall. "A-Two," he breathed.

A-Two's head whipped up. At the same time, her hand clutched at her chest. "You! Thomas!" she said. The drawstring around the neck of her shift was pulled tight, her breasts no longer revealed. "What are you doing here?"

"Milk." Thomas could barely utter the word.

A-Two's face clouded with disgust. "Oh, all right," she conceded, and she fastened her petticoat. "I'll go get it."

"I don't think she was glad to see you," Rosemary volunteered.

But Thomas, deaf to Rosemary, gazed out the

45

back doorway after A-Two. He leaned forward like a flower waiting for sunlight.

But it was Rosemary's mother who returned through the doorway; it was Rosemary's mother who brought the milk. "And butter," said Althea. "A-Two is fetching butter from the springhouse. She made it yesterday. And I'll be making cheese soon. Tell your mother that she'll have a share of that."

"We're grateful." Thomas had found his voice again. "Ma's ever so grateful. Come fall we'll have our own cow. I'm working three days a week at the squire's. He has a good young heifer, old enough to give milk next spring."

"I'm glad to hear that," Althea responded warmly.

A-Two returned with the butter wrapped in sycamore leaves; her hair was almost tamed. Althea poured milk into Thomas's bucket, wrapped the sycamore leaves more firmly around the butter, and handed both to Thomas.

"Thank you, ma'am."

Rosemary followed him outside. "Love!" she trilled melodiously before he was entirely out of hearing.

46

"Oh, shut your mouth," A-Two said crossly.

"I don't want to hear any quarreling," Althea ordered. "Rosemary, bring that bowl inside. A-Two, your father has a task for you today. I think it will include Rosemary."

"Oh, good!" said Rosemary.

"Oh, no!" said A-Two.

"No quarreling," Althea reminded them. "If you wear a disagreeable face now, A-Two, it's going to stay with you for the rest of your life. Your father wants you to take two piglets to Squire Chalmers."

"Piglets!" A-Two began to complain. Then she reconsidered the task: "Squire Chalmers?"

"If you wish, you may stay and visit with Caroline."

A-Two smiled. Then she saw Rosemary. "Why does Rosie have to come?"

"Can you carry two piglets all by yourself?" Althea asked.

"Well, hurry up, then," A-Two said to Rosemary. "Go get the piglets!"

The pigs, like the chickens, roamed freely in the forest. Tending to them was one of Con's special chores. Rosemary went in search of

Con. She found her sister sitting on a steep bank above the river, in a place where the beech trees grew high and strong. Con sat against a tree trunk that was as large around as the chicken house. Rosemary sat down beside her.

"Are you thinking to the Indian?" Rosemary asked.

She had to wait for a long, long minute before Con finally sighed and looked her way. "He's gone," said Con. "What do you want?"

"I didn't see him."

Con waited.

"I think he's short," Rosemary ventured.

"He's taller than you," said Con.

"And old."

"Not as old as Papa."

"Papa says that he must always stay on the other side of the river. I heard Papa tell you so."

Con shrugged.

Rosemary decided to try another approach. "When you think, do you talk?" she asked. "What do you talk about?"

"Nothing," said Con. But then she added,

more kindly, "Everything. We talk about everything that is."

This time it was Rosemary's turn to sigh. "Not even I understand you."

Con's smile was gentle. "Shall I read you a story? Would you like to hear *King Lear*?"

"Yes, please!"

" 'Enter Kent, Gloucester, and Edmund,' " Con began. " 'Kent: I thought the King had more affected the Duke of Albany than Cornwall . . .' "

Rosemary relaxed against the tree. She listened, seeing—but not really seeing—the pages slowly turning in the big bound volume that her mother kept on a special table. Althea owned three books, books that Rosemary's grandmother had owned, and her great-grandmother before that. Rosemary sometimes looked in the books, but too often the words had more letters than her name. A-Two never even glanced at the books.

But Con had read them all, most often from a distance. Sometimes Rosemary would be alone in the house, and she would walk by the table to see that one of the books had been pulled away from the others and opened. Slowly, very slowly, the pages would turn, as if blown by a breath from far away.

" 'We have this hour a constant will to publish our daughters' several dowers . . . ,' " Con now read.

Sometimes, when Rosemary saw those pages turning, she would run into the forest so that she could find Con and sit and listen. Sometimes she would stand still, close her eyes, and think hard, trying to warn Con that their father was soon coming home. If he knew, he would forbid this kind of reading. Rosemary never knew if Con heard her thoughts; but the moment Colin's foot touched the porch, the book always closed by itself and quietly slid back into place.

" 'Tell me, my daughters (since now we will divest us both of rule, interest of territory, cares of state), which of you shall we say doth love us most?' "

"Ro-sie!" This time it was A-Two's impatience traveling from the distance.

Con stopped. "What does she want?"

"Piglets. I forgot."

"Papa's piglets. He told me this morning. I'll call them now." Con peered into the forest. Rosemary peered with her. At first Rosemary saw only beech trunks, smooth and gray. Then she saw an approaching curve of brown; she saw the ground leaves rise into two small mounds. A moment later the mother pig, huge and fierce, was glowering at Rosemary. The two little pigs rushed toward Con. Con stopped the piglets with her hands; she stared at the mother pig. The mother pig, against all reason, against all nature, turned her back on girls and babies and walked away.

"Whew!" said Rosemary.

Con stroked the piglets. "Can you carry them both?"

"I'll try. It's not far."

"Carry them like this." Con draped the little animals over Rosemary's hips; she tucked Rosemary's arms around their bodies.

Rosemary turned toward home. But then she looked back. "Will he return?" she asked. "Your friend?"

"He will," said Con.

51

A-Two stood waiting on the front stoop. She had combed, braided, and wound her hair around her head so that it looked like a crown. She wore her second-best petticoat; her stays were laced tightly over her shift; her very best bodice fit smoothly over her stays.

Rosemary stood still with admiration.

"I've been waiting forever!" said A-Two. "You look terrible! Go comb your hair."

Rosemary set the piglets down and went inside to obey. A-Two followed her. "And wear a petticoat!"

"But it's summer!" Rosemary complained.

"You're old enough to dress decently. Here, give me that comb." A-Two braided Rosemary's hair. "I suppose you'll do."

"You're not going to wear your best apron, are you?" asked Rosemary.

"Why shouldn't I?"

"Piglets," said Rosemary.

"Piglets," A-Two agreed. She covered her own apron with one belonging to Con. "All right. Let's go."

The little pigs were investigating the garden;

they had never seen civilization before. Rosemary picked up the smaller and held it with both hands against her belly. A-Two wrapped her piglet in Con's apron. Holding it well away from her body, she marched down the wagon path. She walked ahead of Rosemary, as if she were all alone, unrelated to her sister—all the way to the squire's turnoff, up the squire's track, to the squire's front gate and walk. Then she unwrapped her piglet and handed it over.

"I can't carry both!" said Rosemary.

"You carried both from Con to the house," said A-Two.

Rosemary shifted the piglets, once again draping them over her hips. A-Two wadded up Con's apron and hid it under a bush. "Come on, now," she said, and she opened the gate.

Ladylike, refined, but barefoot, A-Two minced over a gravel walk that felt like the river bottom to Rosemary's equally bare feet. Rosemary clutched the piglets to her sides and looked hard. She didn't often have the chance to see the front of the squire's house. If it really was a house. It looked more like a king's castle, with stone steps, a big oak door, and a chimney at each end. The house had two floors, and each floor was divided into rooms, and each room had a window with real glass. Rosemary wasn't sure that even King Lear lived so well.

"A-Two!" That was fat Caroline, leaning out of a window on the second floor.

"Caroline!" A-Two called back.

"Come up!"

"Take the piglets around to Seth," A-Two ordered in a low voice.

"Papa said that *you* were to bring the piglets to the squire."

"*You* do it," A-Two said between her teeth.

"A-Two!" called Caroline.

"If I do it," bargained Rosemary, "then I get to do whatever I want during the rest of our time here."

"Fine!" A-Two snapped. Then, recomposing herself, she sang out, "I'm coming, Caroline!"

Satisfied, Rosemary went in search of Seth. She found neither him, the squire, nor anybody else, so she settled the piglets into an empty pen. "Wait here, Goneril," she said. "You too, Regan." She circled back to the front of the house and again walked down the gravel path, this time with her eyes closed, feeling the riverbed with her toes. When her toes touched the stone steps, she opened her eyes. Caroline's window was still open. Try as she might, Rosemary could hear nothing from inside.

Rosemary considered the oak door. She looked down at her feet. She sat down, rubbed her feet with her petticoat, and then stood again.

She had never before pushed open the squire's front door. It was surprisingly heavy. Inside, the wooden floors were smooth and shiny. Rosemary looked into the room on the left, then the room on the right, and then she tiptoed down the hall. She heard voices now, but they came from the kitchen, a low brick building that was stuck onto the back of the house like a handle.

The stairs were in a back parlor, a room made remarkable by a mirror. Rosemary had never seen such a mirror before: as big as a tabletop, set like a window into the wall. Rosemary approached it and then stepped back. She felt strange: very close, and yet very far away; very large, and yet very small.

She continued upward. Upstairs she found eight rooms, two above each downstairs parlor. Rosemary looked into all the empty ones before she opened the door to Caroline's room. She saw A-Two and Caroline lying stomach down on a high bed with a wooden pole at each corner. They were studying a book. Rosemary stepped silently over the threshold.

"I'm sure of it," said A-Two. "The gown is all one piece."

"The bodice isn't separate?" Caroline asked.

"No," A-Two replied. "You can tell by the way the gown drapes. It does have a pretty flow. Twenty yards of cloth, I would guess. Can you imagine? All that cloth for one gown!"

Rosemary tiptoed closer. While A-Two talked, she was jabbing her finger at a drawing that took up a whole page of the book. It was a very ugly drawing, Rosemary thought, of a lady standing between a stone wall and a shrunken tree that had been clipped to look like a dog. The lady's head was tiny, her ankles long, and her gown huge.

"Could you make it?" Caroline asked.

A-Two wriggled her toes and considered. "I

think so," she finally said. "I'd have to figure out how to sew the top to the skirt, though."

"Could you make it for *me*?"

A-Two turned away from the book to look at her friend. In doing so, she noticed Rosemary. "Rosie!"

"You said I could do whatever I wanted," Rosemary said quickly.

"I didn't say you could come up here!"

Caroline laughed. "I don't mind, A-Two. The house is so quiet right now, there really isn't much for her to do."

Feeling invited, Rosemary climbed up onto the bed beside her sister.

Caroline tapped the book. "If I can get Mama to buy enough muslin for two gowns— one for me and one for you—will you make this for me?"

A-Two caught her breath. "Forty yards of cloth! Would your mama buy that much?"

"There's to be a ball in New Bern in July. And you know why I want to go."

A-Two might have known the reason, but Rosemary did not. She made herself very small and very quiet.

"I want him to notice me," said Caroline.

"What if your mama says you can't go?" A-Two asked.

"I'll tell her that I want to visit Mrs. Sitwell."

Sitwell Female Academy. Rosemary remembered: Last winter Caroline had traveled all the way to New Bern to go to school. She had brought home a guitar upon which she had learned to strum a few chords.

"It will need lace." A-Two was all business now. "Probably a yard of lace for each yard of cloth. Will your mama buy lace, too?"

"She'll buy anything," said Caroline, "if she thinks it will make me look pretty."

"But will she also buy lace for *me*?" A-Two asked.

"You're my best friend. And you're going to make my gown. You're the only person I know who can."

"All right," said A-Two. "Let's decide about the sleeves."

Rosemary slipped off the bed. Caroline's guitar lay on a chair beside the window. Rosemary longed to touch it but didn't dare. Instead, she leaned out the window. She looked up and down the track for a long time before she finally saw something. She settled her chin into her hands and waited. It was a cloud of dust; it was a man on a horse; it was two men, on two horses, racing. The man behind caught up, then almost passed the first. Neck and neck, they galloped past the squire's gate. They pulled to a stop and began arguing.

"It was I who was first," said the squire.

"You lost, Father," said the younger man. "Admit it!"

"I admit," said the squire, "that I am the better man."

"But you still lost," said Rosemary.

The two men looked up at the window.

"Hello," she said.

"Rosie, who is out there?" A-Two asked.

"The squire and his son," Rosemary replied.

"And who might you be, sweet maiden?" said the young man, and he did something that Rosemary had never seen a man do before. He took off his hat—a green hat with a blue feather—and, still seated on his horse, swept his arm and body into a low bow.

"Move over," said A-Two.

"Papa!" called Caroline.

Rosemary was almost squeezed from the window.

"But, oh!" gasped the young man. "What beauty breaks in yonder window?"

"It's just me," Caroline giggled. "And my friend, A-Two."

"*Et tu?*" said the young man. "As in the Latin? No. *Étude*, as in the French. *Étude*—a study of beauty."

Before Rosemary's very eyes, her sister melted like sugar.

"Philip," said Caroline. "You're embarrassing my friend!"

"I must meet this beauty!" Philip cried.

Rosemary burrowed between the older girls until she could hang out the window again. "Squire!" she called. "We brought the piglets."

"I hate you," A-Two said later, when she and Rosemary were walking home. "I hate you, hate you, hate you!"

"All I did was tell him about the piglets," Rosemary defended herself.

A-Two was walking backward, so that she

could hate Rosemary face-to-face. "But you knew who he was. You knew that the squire had a son! Philip!"

"Seth told me."

"You didn't tell me!"

"I forgot."

"I hate you." A-Two whipped her body around.

"What would you have done if I had told you?" Rosemary asked her sister's spine.

Bitterly, A-Two replied, "I would have worn shoes."

CHAPTER 4

A Baby

Benjie-from-the-smith's stood importantly in the very middle of Rosemary's house. He stood like a soldier with his chest out and his chin high—one of General Washington's warriors. A man, in his own eyes. A snail, to Rosemary.

"Motherwort," said Althea. "Liferoot. Skullcap. Rosemary oil. Rosemary!"

"Yes, Mama," said Rosemary, and she stopped glaring at Benjie.

"I'll need some birthwort. Probably not tonight, but possibly tomorrow morning. I'll want you to bring me some."

"Yes, Mama."

"A-Two!"

"Yes, Mama." A-Two put down the gown she was sewing.

"You'll be in charge of the house. That means extra work for you."

"Yes, Mama."

"I think we should go now," Benjie said manfully. "Miller's wife did say that Mrs. DiAngeli's time was almost here."

"You don't even know what that means," taunted Rosemary. "Do you? Do you?"

"I'm sure there's time to spare," said Althea. "There always is with the first one." She went to the back door and looked out. Rosemary slipped under her mother's arm and looked with her. Con and Colin sat on opposite ends of the porch, their faces almost identical profiles in the dimming light. "A-Two will feed you," said Althea. "I do hope that the haying goes well tomorrow."

"Thank you, wife," said Colin.

Con just nodded.

"Benjie?" said Althea. Benjie sprang to attention. "We'll go."

They left with Benjie leading and Althea carrying her bundle. Rosemary watched her mother fade into the early dusk. The fireflies were still low, no higher than Rosemary's knees, their glow made pale by what remained of the day's light. Rosemary remembered her chickens.

When she returned to the house, A-Two was still sewing, but now by the light of a candle. Rosemary touched the cloth.

"Stop it!" Hardly missing a stitch, A-Two slapped at her sister's hand.

"It's pretty," Rosemary said. "But not pretty enough to make Caroline pretty."

"Hmph."

Rosemary sat on the floor, as close as she could without touching the cloth, and looked at it. Caroline and her mother had chosen a fabric that would have been perfectly white except for the tiny blue flowers that had been scattered like corn, sometimes landing singly, sometimes in little clumps. Rosemary tried to name the flowers—Quaker lady, dayflower, blue-eyed grass? These flowers were like none she had ever seen.

"You're sitting on it!" said A-Two.

"I'm not!" Rosemary protested.

A-Two sighed. "Read to me," she ordered. Rosemary obediently stood and went to the little table where the books lay. She began to open the volume about Zeus and Demeter and all the nymphs. "No," said A-Two, "the Bible."

Rosemary opened the Bible instead.

"The Song of Solomon," A-Two directed.

"Again?"

"Again," said A-Two. And while Rosemary read, A-Two also mouthed the words. " 'A bundle of myrrh is my well-beloved unto me; he shall lie all night betwixt my breasts. . . .' "

The next morning, when Benjie invaded Rosemary's house, he demanded a second breakfast, which was, it turned out, really his third. "Ate early," he said, "at home. And then went up to the old schoolhouse, where the cooper lives. Your mama gave me some ham and told me to tell you that she wants some trillium root, too. Not just birthwort. I like your corn bread just fine, miss." He smiled at A-Two.

A-Two, like Rosemary, was unimpressed. "No more for you," she said. "The rest is for those of us who have to work today. Shouldn't you be haying?"

"Yes," said Benjie. "But this is more fun."

A-Two snorted. "Go on, Rosie," she said. "You'd better go to Mama."

Benjie followed Rosemary into the forest— like an unwanted dog, she thought. But unlike a dog, he talked constantly. "That's ginger that you're pulling up," he pointed out. "Your mama said birthwort."

"It's a *kind* of ginger." Rosemary spoke from the lofty level of experience. "Birthwort is a kind of ginger."

"My cousin Hammond," said Benjie, "crushes up ginger leaves and then puts them inside his shirt when he goes courting, so that he'll smell good."

"For *that*," Rosemary informed her companion, "you use the pointy-leafed ginger." She paused. "A-Two does it, too."

"Who's courting A-Two now?"

"Thomas Small seems to like her."

"I like Thomas," Benjie approved.

"A-Two doesn't. Not much."

"Who does she like?" Benjie inquired. "My cousin Hammond says she's particular. Won't have just any beau."

"Well, I think she likes . . ." For a moment

Rosemary stopped, both in her search for trillium and in her speech. She didn't want to reveal too much about her family life. But there was something about A-Two's new choice that bothered her, something Rosemary could not yet describe. "She likes Philip Chalmers. Look, here's the trillium."

"Chalmers!" Benjie squatted beside Rosemary while she dug and pulled. "Him?"

"He wears shoes," Rosemary explained.

"And a red coat! And a waistcoat embroidered with flowers! He *looks* like a flower. He smells like one, too."

"He does?"

"Last week he came to my pa—new shoes for that mare of his. I stood right beside him."

"And he smelled like a flower?"

"No flower that I could give a name to. But if I was a bee, I'd be interested."

Rosemary sat back on her heels. "He talks French." It was the only defense she could offer for her sister's choice.

"Thomas Small can fell three trees in a day," Benjie returned.

Rosemary nodded. Of the two talents, it was obvious which was the more useful.

"Do you have all you need?" said Benjie. "Are you ready? Your mama is waiting."

The women from the mill had already arrived at the schoolhouse. Mr. DiAngeli stood nervously waiting outside, supported in both manhood and exclusion by Mr. Algernon Proctor, Mrs. Olivia Proctor's young husband. Benjie joined the men. Rosemary stepped over the threshold and into the female domain.

She hadn't been inside the schoolhouse since that winter, two years before, when she went to school. Now it looked much like her own home. The log benches were gone; the lean-to, at the back of the building, held a big cupboard. There was a table next to the fireplace, and a big bed in the corner farthest from the door.

Mrs. DiAngeli lay on the bed with her stomach hiding her face. The miller's wife held her hand. "Pull hard against me, Mrs. DiAngeli," the miller's wife was saying. "Pull hard when you next feel the pain."

"Wash and trim a trillium root, Rosie," Althea directed. She knelt at Mrs. DiAngeli's feet.

"Hello, Rosie," said Mrs. Olivia Proctor. She stood on Mrs. DiAngeli's other side, her arm caught in Mrs. DiAngeli's grip. Silent Miss Nancy Proctor stood beside Althea, a pile of swaddling clothes in her hands.

Rosemary went to work. She prepared the trillium root, which she gave to her mother, and which her mother gave to Mrs. DiAngeli to chew. She built up the fire—although the room was already warm—and boiled a kettle of bathwater with tansy, camomile, and mint. She listened to Mrs. DiAngeli's moans, her mother's orders, the other women's encouragements. She saw the big belly on the bed move like earth disturbed by a mole. She brought the kettle to her mother; she began making a tea of birthwort and motherwort. She heard Mrs. DiAngeli's screams, the other women's gasps as the pregnant lady pulled against them, and then the surprising voice of Miss Nancy Proctor saying, "It's here, Mrs. DiAngeli. The child has come."

Rosemary went to look. Althea was waiting for the afterbirth, but Mrs. Olivia Proctor was already cleaning the baby with water from Rosemary's kettle. "A little boy!" Mrs. Olivia Proctor said softly. "A perfect little boy."

"Look, Mrs. DiAngeli," said the miller's wife, and Mrs. DiAngeli looked.

"Ohhh!" she sighed, and the pain on her face wonderfully disappeared.

"Bring Mrs. DiAngeli the tea," said Althea.

Rosemary obeyed. By the time she brought the tea, Mrs. DiAngeli was propped against pillows and holding her baby to her breast. Her face was alight with joy. She showed no interest in the cup Rosemary offered.

"Drink the tea," Althea ordered. "It will help to stop the bleeding."

Reluctantly, Mrs. DiAngeli handed her baby back to Mrs. Olivia Proctor.

Rosemary opened the door and poked her head outside. The two men and Benjie sat in a row on one of the discarded school benches. Mr. DiAngeli looked as if he had been folded up by fear. "Maria stopped screaming," he whispered. "Is she dead?"

"She had a baby," said Rosemary. "It's a boy."

"A boy." And Mr. DiAngeli began to unfold. He turned to Mr. Algernon Proctor. He grasped his friend's hand. "A boy!"

Rosemary closed the door; she held it shut with her back; she waited. Mrs. Olivia Proctor was crooning to the baby. Althea was bathing Mrs. DiAngeli with the warm water. The other women were tidying up the room.

"He's beautiful," Mrs. DiAngeli said dreamily. "Isn't he."

From outside the house there came a war whoop and then a bellowing shout: "It's a boy!"

"I have three boys," said the miller's wife, "and every single one is beautiful."

There was a pounding at the door.

"Mama?" Rosemary asked.

"She's ready," said Althea, and Rosemary stood aside.

The man who strode through the doorway was no longer a man made small by fear. Instead, Mr. DiAngeli walked as though he were as tall as the rafters. "A son!" he announced.

"For you, Flavio," said his wife.

"A son . . ." Now Mr. DiAngeli's voice was gentle. He very carefully peered at the bundle in Mrs. Olivia Proctor's arms. He very tenderly leaned over to kiss his wife. He stood tall again. "I want to explode!"

"Shhh!" Miss Nancy Proctor warned.

"Go outside," laughed the miller's wife. "Go outside and do some hard work. That will settle you."

"We should return to haying," said Mr. Algernon Proctor.

"No," said Mr. DiAngeli. "I will go into the forest, to the land that I have marked as my own. I will begin to build a farm for my son!"

Mr. Algernon Proctor slapped the cooper's back. "I'll go get my ax," he offered.

"I'll help!" said Benjie.

When the men were gone, Mrs. DiAngeli spoke shyly from her bed. "If you look in that cupboard, Mrs. Weston," she said, "or you, Rosemary, if you look on the bottom shelf, you will see a bottle of wine. My husband's mother gave it to me to offer to you ladies after the birth."

Rosemary opened the cupboard, found five

cups, and poured the wine. She poured a full cup for her mother, a half cup for the other ladies, and a fingernail's depth for herself.

"Well," said the miller's wife, coming to the table, "our Rosemary knows how to split the pay according to the work."

"There's still a half bottle left," said Mrs. Olivia Proctor.

While Mrs. DiAngeli dozed in the big bed, her baby in her arms, the ladies drank. At first they sipped decorously, making polite comments about the superior wine and the superior baby they had just brought into the world. They called each other Mrs. and Miss. By the time they got to the second pouring, they had relaxed all the way down to first names.

"What's your A-Two doing today, Althea?" asked the miller's wife. "She is turning out to be a pretty girl."

"Haying," said Althea. "And cooking."

"And praying," Rosemary volunteered. "She prays every evening now."

"Of course she prays," said the miller's wife. And then, as an afterthought: "What does she pray?"

"The Song of Solomon," answered Rosemary. "All eight stanzas."

"Oh!" whooped the miller's wife. Rosemary was startled: All the ladies were laughing.

"Oh, I do remember!" said the miller's wife.

"The Song of Solomon, eight days in a row," said Mrs. Olivia Proctor, "and on the ninth night you will see the face of your beau."

"In my time," said the miller's wife, "we used to take a mirror and a candle and walk down the stairs backward. Oh, the tumbles we had! But it was the same thing—on the last step, if you made it there, you would see the face of the man you were to marry."

"I always ate the point of a piece of pie first," said Miss Nancy Proctor. "You always told me, Mother, that it would make me an old maid." She looked shyly at the others. "I wanted to be an old maid."

"When I was young," said the miller's wife, "I poured the white of an egg into a glass of water. The idea, you see, was to give me a picture of the man I would marry."

"And what did you see?" Althea asked.

"A fat blob. Which, of course, was impossible. I was already in love with your father, Nancy, and he was a nice, slim young man. But in the last several years he's grown quite a belly, hasn't he! The egg told the truth after all."

The three women from the mill laughed and laughed. Althea smiled over their heads at Rosemary.

"Country magic," said the miller's wife, wiping the tears from her face. "Simple stuff. Sometimes the preachers warned us against it. But oh, it was fun!"

"I don't think A-Two is having fun," said Rosemary.

"Of course not," said Mrs. Olivia Proctor. "She's seventeen, she's serious. She thinks she's doing something about her future. More wine, Mother?"

"Of course," said the miller's wife.

"I should go home," said Althea. "I should be haying."

"We should all be haying," said Mrs. Olivia Proctor. "Everybody from the smith's is haying. Mrs. Bathsheba said *that* is why she couldn't help us today."

"You are speaking about our neighbor," warned the miller's wife, but her chiding wasn't forceful.

"You would think that a *Christian*—," Mrs. Olivia Proctor started to say. But at that moment the door opened and Benjie flew through. He was breathing hard, his face was wild, his voice was high with fear.

"Mrs. Weston!" he cried. "Oh, Mrs. Weston!"

"Out of the way, boy!" Mr. Algernon Proctor commanded, and he pushed past Benjie with what looked to be a sack of blood slung over his shoulder. Except that the sack was a body, and the blood was streaming from the creature's head.

"On the floor!" Althea ordered. She was already kneeling. When the head was close to her hands, she pushed her thumbs hard into the little depressions before each ear.

"What is it?" asked Mrs. DiAngeli sleepily. "Is something wrong?"

Rosemary opened her mother's bundle of herbs. She found the rosemary oil and the powder from the puffball mushroom. She held them tightly and waited. Benjie was crying.

"What is it?" Mrs. DiAngeli asked again, but nobody answered her. They were all silent, watching.

"Cover him," said Althea.

Miss Nancy Proctor immediately produced a quilt.

The creature turned its head, just a little, and moaned.

"Flavio?" said Mrs. DiAngeli.

The blood that had been rushing like water through a sluice gate ebbed, and then stopped.

"All right," said Althea, and her shoulders dropped.

"Flavio!" said Mrs. DiAngeli. Mrs. Olivia Proctor moved toward the bed.

"Is he alive?" asked Mr. Algernon Proctor.

"He is." Althea's answer was short. "Bring me the wash water, Nancy."

"Here's the rosemary oil, Mama." Rosemary opened her hands at her mother's side.

"Boil some comfrey," Althea directed. "And then boil some willow bark and camomile."

"Yes, Mama." Rosemary built up the fire again.

"How did it happen, son?" asked the miller's wife.

"Logging," said Mr. Algernon Proctor. "It wasn't a large tree, and we thought it would fall free. But it hit an oak limb. The limb fell. DiAngeli was right below."

"I tried to save him." Benjie sniffled. "I yelled!"

"It happened so fast," said Mr. Algernon Proctor. "There was nothing we could do."

"You brought him here," said Althea. "That may have been enough."

After Rosemary finished her tasks, Althea sent her home. Rosemary stood in the doorway, looking back. Mrs. DiAngeli lay weeping, her baby forgotten beside her. The miller's wife was making a bed for Mr. DiAngeli on the floor. Althea laid a poultice over Mr. DiAngeli's forehead while Miss Nancy Proctor continued to wash the blood from his chest and arms. Mrs. Olivia and Mr. Algernon Proctor stood against a wall, staring. There was a trail of blood all the way to the door.

The trail of blood continued outside, where Benjie was following it like a forlorn hound. "I yelled," he told Rosemary when she came near. "I really yelled." And then, as she passed by: "But there was nothing anybody could have done."

Rosemary didn't believe him.

All the way home she didn't believe him. She stomped down the wagon path with anger, and the first person she saw was A-Two. A-Two was drawing a big circle in the dust of the yard with the handle of a frying pan—another attempt to foresee the face of her intended.

"It won't work," Rosemary snapped. "You're not like Con."

"I can try," A-Two snapped back. And then she saw Rosemary's face. "Is something wrong?" she asked. "Did the baby die?"

"The baby," said Rosemary, "*did not die!*" And she flung herself inside the house.

A-Two followed after. "Was it the mother, then? Are you sick, Rosie?"

"*I am not sick!*"

"Sit down." With little backward glances at Rosemary, A-Two poured some cool water from a jug. She placed the mug before her sister. "It's a hot day to walk along that road," she observed.

And at this unaccustomed sweetness from A-Two, Rosemary—like Benjie before her—broke down and cried.

Althea didn't come home until the following evening, when the fireflies had already begun to rise. She told her news, briefly, at the supper table. Then, when the older girls began to wash up, she went out to her garden.

Rosemary followed. She knelt beside her mother and, like her mother, pulled weeds. Twilight covered their hands. "Will he really be all right?"

"He will live," Althea answered.

"But will he be all right?"

Althea paused. "I don't know."

"You could have saved him," Rosemary accused.

"I stopped him from dying."

"No," said Rosemary, and she ended her pretense at weeding. "No, that's not enough. Anybody could have done that. You've even showed me how. You just press where the blood pumps are. You could have stopped that limb from falling!"

"Not from a distance," Althea reminded her daughter. "I'm not like Con. I have to be there. I have to see it."

"You could have helped!" Rosemary almost shouted. And then she was sobbing. "They were so happy!"

Althea also stopped weeding. "Listen to me, Rosie, and listen carefully. There are many things that I cannot do. But more especially, most of what I can do, I cannot do in front of people. It would frighten them. It would be dangerous for me."

"No," Rosemary argued.

"I will say one thing more," Althea continued, "and then we will end this discussion. You heard the ladies talk about a kind of magic yesterday: a false magic, a wish magic. It's silly stuff; I've never heard that it works. But it frequently does harm. It does harm because it is born of desires; it focuses the mind upon desires. To be controlled by one's desires is an evil thing. Remember that, Rosie."

Althea waited, silently but firmly, forcing Rosemary to speak.

"Yes, Mama," Rosemary finally uttered, reluctantly.

Althea put her hands back to the earth. The fireflies were above her head now. The boldest were above the trees. Rosemary stood and walked through their light. She went to the chicken house, to think.

CHAPTER 5

Beaux

It was two nights later that the family ate Chloe for supper. Rosemary did not share in her father's grace. She bowed her head, as Colin had directed. But instead of listening to his prayers, she talked to Chloe's ghost. She begged pardon for what her mother had done—killing Chloe. She promised to make the most of Chloe's sustenance; she promised to do honor to Chloe's chicken soul.

"Amen," said Colin.

"Amen," said Rosemary.

"Papa," said A-Two, "I've almost finished Caroline's gown."

"Good!" Colin approved.

"And Mama said that if you agreed, I could spend the day with Caroline tomorrow—fitting the gown, I mean. Rosie can do my work here. It's just potatoes that have to be dug."

Rosemary's head shot up from Chloe's drumstick.

"I think that would be fine," said Colin.

"Potatoes?" Rosemary protested. "All day?"

"Half of the day," Althea compromised, "in the morning, while it's still cool. You can spend the afternoon in the forest, gathering herbs."

Rosemary felt abused.

The next morning, her knees and her hands thick with dirt and her digging stick momentarily forgotten, she watched A-Two leave the house. This time A-Two was dressed in her best of everything: best petticoat, best bodice. Her stays were pulled so tight that her breasts almost poked up over her bodice. She carried a thick package wrapped in clean old muslin, with a lump on top. The package, Rosemary knew, was Caroline's gown. The lump, she surmised, was A-Two's shoes.

She watched silently, and balefully, as A-Two disappeared down the wagon path. Then, with a ferocity almost equal to the growing heat of the day, Rosemary dug potatoes. She piled potato upon potato until she had created a pyramid as high as her waist. She stood and yelled for her mother. "Mama!"

Althea shot out of the house. "What?" she shouted. "What?"

"Is this enough?"

"Oh, Rosie!" Althea paused as if to scold, but then changed her mind. "Yes, that's more than enough."

As a reward, or perhaps an apology, Althea prepared a walking meal for her daughter: bread, butter, and as many strawberries as Rosemary could hold in her hand.

Rosemary, freed, wandered into the forest. She walked into a chorus of cicada song, a round with one wave of song blending into the next. She tried to sing along but couldn't: Her voice was too different for imitation. Usually Rosemary was pleased by the difference; today she was annoyed. She gathered the white Indian-pipe flowers her mother had requested, and turned toward civilization.

Pushing through the low-slung branches of

cedar trees, she emerged at the far end of the squire's peach orchard. There she saw Thomas Small working with Black Seth. The two stood with their backs to Rosemary; they were examining a young, green fruit.

"The squire could lose them all," said Thomas.

"I can get you the soot," said Seth. "And I think the squire has a barrel of quicklime."

Without their notice, Rosemary passed them by. She set her flowers down at the very edge of the orchard. Then she stood to admire the back of the squire's mansion. She counted eight windows, each with fifteen panes of glass. The squire's back door was almost as large as his front door. And instead of a back porch, the door opened onto brick steps. The steps dropped gracefully to a large square of carefully tended lawn with a sundial in the middle.

The sight of those steps reawakened a question in Rosemary's mind: If the squire and his family didn't wash up on a back porch, how did they keep themselves from tracking dirt inside? As she approached the steps, Rosemary smoothed her hair down with her hands. She brushed off the sole of each foot against its opposite leg.

When she entered the house, she was as silent as a moth. She heard footsteps, heavy footsteps; she stood still. She heard a little grunt as the heavy person sat: the squire's wife. By Rosemary's calculations, the lady sat in the room adjacent to the room that held the mirror and the stairs.

Rosemary wafted up the stairs. She touched the latch on Caroline's door and pushed. There was Caroline, standing in the middle of the floor with her mouth pinched and her chest high, as if she were stopping herself from breathing. There was A-Two, kneeling at Caroline's side with pins in her mouth and her hands pulling Caroline's waist as tight as possible.

A-Two spit out the pins. "Rosie!"

"Mama didn't say that I couldn't come." Rosemary swiftly pulled the door shut behind her. She paused, thinking of the diplomatic thing to say. "The gown is very pretty."

And it was pretty, with sleeves gathered at both elbow and wrist, and a higher-than-usual waist covering most of Caroline's plumpness.

"Do you think so?" Caroline asked.

"Ignore her!" said A-Two.

"It makes you look like . . . like you're taller, but smaller," Rosemary answered tactfully. "I think the sleeves are pretty, too."

"The sleeves were A-Two's idea. She didn't even see them in a pattern book. She made them up all by herself."

Rosemary smiled at A-Two, more a smile of victory than a compliment.

A-Two snorted. "Oh, all right. You can stay. But you have to help."

For the next hour Rosemary did as her sister directed. She pulled stay strings; she held gathers together; she basted yards and yards of hem. When the gown was almost finished, she followed the older girls downstairs. The squire's wife sat before a window with an embroidery frame angled toward the light.

"Mama?" said Caroline.

"Oh, love!" The embroidery frame was pushed aside. The squire's wife rose to walk all the way around her blushing daughter. Rosemary and A-Two stepped back into the wallpaper. The squire's ladies were very large. The older woman clasped her hands together. "So elegant! You look," and she sounded almost sad, "so grown up."

"I am grown up," said Caroline. "I'm quite grown up now."

"It's lovely," the squire's wife pronounced. "And you, A-Two—" She peered into the recesses of the room; A-Two stepped forward. "—have done beautiful work."

"I hope the gown that you make for yourself," said Caroline, "will be as pretty as mine."

The squire's two ladies smiled at each other with mutual satisfaction. "Let's have tea!" the squire's wife suggested. She sat down again with her embroidery. "Rosie, run and tell Tillie that we want tea."

Being the only person in the room without shoes, Rosemary was almost glad to leave it. She found Tillie, the indentured girl, alone in the kitchen. Half the table was covered with flour; Rosemary leaned against the clean end. "Are you making bread?" she asked.

"Bread," said Tillie, "and cakes, and pies, and cobblers. Do you know how much these people eat? Each one of them—excepting Master Philip, of course—eats as much in one day as a whole family would eat for a week in my village in Ireland."

"Oh," said Rosemary. Now that she looked closely at Tillie, it did seem that Tillie was remarkably thin. "Why did the people in your village eat so little?"

Tillie looked at Rosemary as though Rosemary were remarkably stupid. "Because they were starving."

Rosemary had no reply to that.

"What do you want?" said Tillie.

"Tea," Rosemary answered. "For Caroline and Mrs. Squire, and I suppose for my sister, too."

When Rosemary left the kitchen, she walked very carefully. She carried the tray that Tillie had prepared: hot water, milk, cups, saucers, plates, spoons, forks, bread and butter, cake and cobbler. She set the tray down on the floor before she opened any doors. When she walked into the mirror room, she shifted the tray and glanced into the glass: Rosemary, carrying a tray half as large as herself.

She paused before entering the room where the ladies sat. Their voices had been joined by the voices of men.

"There she is!" said the squire's wife. "Run back for two more cups, dear."

"No, no," said the squire. "Philip and I had refreshment in town."

Philip had squeezed himself onto the settee between Caroline and A-Two. Caroline, holding most of her gown on her lap, looked annoyed. A-Two looked as though she had just eaten some of Althea's special mushrooms. "Oh, Philip!" she trilled. He must have said something very clever.

Rosemary looked around, trying to decide what to do with her tray.

"Put it on the little table, dear," the squire's wife directed.

Rosemary did as she was told and then retired with a piece of poppy seed cake to the window-sill behind the embroidery frame. She sat, dangling her legs. She watched; she listened.

"Of course, I hadn't thought to buy two carriages." The squire was expansive. "But you know how persuasive Philip can be, my dear. So the landau will be for you and Caroline—very ladylike. And the phaeton—"

"Can we afford two?" the squire's wife asked placidly.

"The phaeton is faster than the wind!" Philip interjected. "Father will cover everybody with dust!"

"Oh, Philip!" A-Two trilled.

"The landau is slow, but it's bigger," said Philip. "Big enough even for Caroline."

From the top of her bodice to where her hair met her head, Caroline turned red.

Philip smiled at A-Two. "Father and I brought the phaeton back with us," he said coaxingly. "Would you like to come with me for a little drive?"

"Oh—," A-Two began.

"She has to have her tea first," the squire's wife said comfortably. "Don't you, dear?" She took a key from her pocket and, leaning heavily from her chair, opened a little chest from which she took tea and—Rosemary stopped eating—a box of white sugar. She put the tea into the pot and the sugar into three cups. Then, after locking the chest, she poured.

Rosemary felt as thin as Tillie as she watched her sister and the squire's ladies eat and drink, and eat some more. The squire helped himself, generously, to the food on the tray. Philip, rather than eating, talked. He talked about the phaeton, about horses, about racing—about nothing that, to Rosemary's mind, was very important.

When teatime ended, it was again Rosemary's job to return the tray to the kitchen.

"I've brought the tray," she told Tillie.

"I suppose they ate everything," Tillie grumbled. She was leaning into an oven, inspecting her baking bread.

"Well, the squire helped them."

"The squire?" Tillie turned around; she was suddenly smiling. "Then Master Philip is home?" She put her hand to her hair. "Did he say he liked my cake?"

Rosemary left the kitchen filled with thoughts on the subject of Philip, Oh-Philip!

For some reason, he had the ability to turn otherwise difficult young women sweet and stupid. It was a perplexing skill.

Pondering, Rosemary made her way back to the edge of the orchard, to the spot where she had left Althea's flowers. Thomas and Seth were working behind the first row of trees, shoveling soot and quicklime into little piles. Rosemary picked up the flowers and went to inspect their work. "Lots of bugs," she commented as she walked around a tree.

"Not for long," said Seth. "You had better stand out of the way, Rosie."

"I know," Rosemary answered. She was about to continue the conversation, but the squire's voice interrupted her.

"How is it going, Thomas?" he asked. "Think we'll save the fruit?"

Thomas stopped shoveling. "I think so," he said. He and Rosemary looked beyond the squire, to where Philip had draped himself over a low, reaching limb.

"What filthy work!" Philip said with an exaggerated shudder.

"But necessary," said the squire.

"One would have to have no sense of decorum and taste to do a job like that," Philip remarked. He eyed Thomas's soot-covered breeches with contempt.

Thomas, from his side of the tree, eyed Philip's embroidered waistcoat and thin stockings with equal disdain.

"I don't want to interrupt your work," the squire said, and he moved away.

"Rosie," Seth warned, and he gestured with his head so that she too would move away. Rosemary clutched her flowers against her chest and stepped backward.

Philip stayed where he was. "Rosie?" he said incredulously. "*That?* A rose? She's too dirty to be anything but a rat: a scavenger rat. Whatever it is that she's holding, it's probably something she stole."

Rosemary gasped. She would have dropped her flowers and run in for a fight, but she noticed that Thomas had put down his shovel and picked up a bucket of water. With Thomas, she turned her nose into the wind, satisfying herself that it came from the right direction. The squire was half a field away. Seth now stood

95

right beside Rosemary. Thomas checked to see that Seth was clear, and then he tossed his bucket of water onto the mixture of quicklime and soot. A dark, noxious cloud boiled up from the ground to envelop Philip and his tree.

"Aagh!" Philip coughed, sputtered; he tried to swear. He emerged from the cloud with his hands over his eyes and his fine white stockings stained a deep shade of gray. "You savage!" he managed to utter as he turned in a blind circle.

"Oh, Philip!" A-Two's trill carried around the barn and over the field to the orchard.

Philip turned toward her voice like a compass needle turning north. He ran.

"That will be good for the tree," Seth said gravely as he watched Philip stumble through the new corn.

"Kills the insects," Thomas agreed.

Rosemary looked up at Thomas with new respect. She hadn't realized it before, but she liked Thomas Small very much. Very much indeed.

CHAPTER 6

Puck

Slowly, very slowly, Rosemary stepped down the wagon path. She stopped and frowned, again and again, peering into the Queen Anne's lace: big white blossoms with hundreds of flowerlets each, maybe half of the blossoms sporting a tiny purple center. Rosemary plucked the purple flowerlets with a delicate tug and dropped each one into a gourd cup. Althea had said that she needed two spoonfuls. Rosemary would be searching and plucking for a very long time. She frowned into another flower; she blew away a small horde of ants, and—

"Boo!"

Startled, Rosemary dropped her gourd. She turned around with her teeth bared, ready for a fight, but it was only Benjie. Rosemary decided that she wouldn't dignify his presence, not even with a word. She picked up her gourd and let Benjie look at the back of her neck.

"More flowers for your mama?" he asked.

Rosemary blew away another community of ants.

"Never heard of any use for Queen Anne's lace before," said Benjie.

"They're for Mr. DiAngeli," Rosemary, the font of all knowledge, deigned to reply. "For his falling-down sickness. Although they probably won't work."

"Why won't they work? Why are you picking them, then?"

"Because Mr. DiAngeli *thinks* they might work. And if he thinks they work, then maybe they will."

"It doesn't make any sense to me."

It didn't make any sense to Rosemary either, but she didn't choose to say so to Benjie.

"Mr. DiAngeli had another fit yesterday," Benjie said by way of conversation.

Rosemary stopped picking flowerlets. She turned. "What was it like?"

"He was talking to my pa. And all of a sudden, in the middle of a sentence, he dropped down to the ground like this." Benjie demonstrated. "And he threw his arms and legs around like this." Benjie continued his performance. "And his eyes were rolling back, and his mouth was moving like a fish's." By now Benjie was indeed a sight to see, stained and smeared with orange-red dust.

Rosemary was impressed.

"It only lasted a minute, though." Benjie stopped his flailing and gaping and sat up. "He says that he never had fits before, not back in Wilmington, where they used to live. He said he never had a fit until he got hit by that tree."

"Yes." Rosemary sighed sadly.

"You picking the white ones or the purple ones?" Benjie was standing now.

"Purple."

In silence they plucked together.

"Does your sister still like Master Philip?" Benjie asked.

"*Master* Philip?"

"That's what he wants everybody—not just Seth and Tillie—to call him."

Rosemary blew air out of her nose, rudely. "He said that I stole."

"You? What does he think you stole?"

"Flowers."

"Why would you steal flowers?"

"I hate him! I wish he would go away forever! I wish I could throw these flowers in his face and make him go *poof!*" Rosemary was fierce.

"Caroline's gone," said Benjie. "You should have seen her sitting with her mama in that big landau. Six trunks, they had. That's what Seth said. He's driving them to New Bern."

"I wish *Master* Philip had gone with them," Rosemary said bitterly.

"He'll be here for Independence Day. Of that we can be sure," Benjie replied.

They plucked purple hearts until their fingers were cramped from pinching. Then Benjie dropped a final flowerlet into the half-filled gourd and said, "I have to go do other things now. Goodbye." Rosemary looked at their collective harvest: six spoonfuls, at least.

And maidens call it love-in-idleness. The words

floated into her mind. She knew where they came from: A *Midsummer Night's Dream*, one of the stories that Con sometimes read aloud. In the story, love-in-idleness was a flower—a magical flower that made people fall into, or sometimes out of, love. Mostly the story was about love. But the more interesting parts were about magic—and the creatures who wielded that magic. Creatures far more powerful than either Althea or Con. Creatures such as the hobgoblin Puck, who could change things.

The next morning, when Rosemary awoke, she was no longer Rosemary Weston—she was Puck. Puck, who wasn't ordered by rules or family. Puck, who could put a girdle around the world in forty minutes.

She crept down the ladder-stairs from her bedroom loft to examine the Weston family. Colin was the first to get up from the breakfast table. "I'll take the grain to the miller this morning, Althea," he said. "What do you want me to buy?"

Althea also stood. She went to the cupboard. "Coffee," she said. "Salt. Five pounds of sugar."

Puck sighed. The Weston parents were depressingly ordinary. The oldest Weston sister sat like a lump at the table, eating her corn bread with slow deliberation. The second sister had circles of high excitement on both her cheeks. "More sugar, Mama," said A-Two. "I'm making my special cake, for Philip."

Still tucked onto the ladder-stairs, Puck pretended to gag.

"Rosie?" said Althea.

"I'm fine," said Rosemary.

"Do you want to go with your papa?"

"Yes."

"Eat some breakfast first."

"Independence Day tomorrow," Colin said happily, when he and Rosemary were together on the wagon seat. "The salute and the picnic at the mill; then, later, the ball at the squire's. Do you want to carry my shotgun, Rosie? Before the salute?"

"Yes!"

"Jump off here, then." They had reached the track that led to Squire Chalmers's house. "Tell the squire that with Thomas Small we'll have thirteen men but only twelve guns. Ask him if

102

he'll loan Thomas a musket. Then come find me at the mill."

Rosemary found nobody at the squire's: not Philip, not Tillie, not the squire himself. She shouted into the house. She shouted into the kitchen. She shouted into the barn. She thought of one last place to shout—the orchard—and she was walking there when she saw Benjie's bottom sticking out from a bush. "Ben—," she started to say, but a hand poked itself out from the bush and beckoned to her.

As light and invisible as Puck, Rosemary crept into the bushes. The ground was cool: Some of the bushes leaned over a stream. Other bushes leaned against a springhouse, and it was against this springhouse that Benjie had pressed his face. Rosemary did likewise. The structure was made of rough wood; there were plenty of chinks for her to look through.

At first she saw nothing but the darkness of shadow. And she heard almost nothing: the bubble of the water as it sprang from the ground, the silver trickle of its run through the dairy channel. And then a moan.

Rosemary caught her breath. She tried very, very hard to make her eyes focus. And then she could see: Tillie, her face blessed as if by prayer, lying flat on her back with one bare foot dangerously near a milk jug; Philip, lying on top of Tillie with his face pressed against her chest. Tillie's stays were undone. Philip's feet, elegantly shod, dangled in the water of the dairy channel.

Rosemary sat back from the springhouse. She thought. She considered. Benjie, an avid watcher, didn't move. Rosemary punched him in the side. Benjie pinched back. Rosemary took hold of Benjie's hand and pulled him out of the bushes.

"No!" he protested.

"What's that?" Tillie said anxiously.

"Dog," said Philip. "Just a dog."

"What are you doing?" Benjie whispered.

"How long have they been there?" Rosemary whispered back.

"Not long. You should have seen what they did!"

"I know what people do."

"Then why do you look so strange?"

"I'm thinking."

"About what?"

"About how to change the course of history," said Puck.

"What?"

"About how to show A-Two what Philip really is," Rosemary replied.

"How?"

"If I could make her see this . . ." Rosemary waved her hand.

"They're not going to do it in *front* of her!"

"But they might do it again. Tomorrow night. At the ball."

"If they do it," Benjie promised, "I'll be watching. And I'll let you know."

It was just before dawn the next morning when Rosemary and Colin arrived at the mill. They made a small group: thirteen men, plus Rosemary and a gaggle of children who had escaped their homes before breakfast. Everybody looked distant, but close, in the wan, breaking light. With special pride, Rosemary hefted her father's shotgun over her shoulder—a shotgun almost as long as one of her arms, or even one of her legs. She stood one step behind Colin and waited like a soldier herself until the slow-moving sun pushed up over the eastern trees.

"Ready, men!" the squire called out. Colin put his hand behind his back; Rosemary smartly shifted the shotgun over. "Aim!" The twelve old soldiers, plus Thomas, pointed their shotguns and rifles and muskets at the sun. "Fire one!"

It was a loud beginning, a wonderful beginning, a beginning that was probably heard all the way up to Virginia: Independence Day, 1790. With the thirteenth and last round the neighborhood began to gather. Eventually Althea and A-Two arrived with the wagon.

"Rosie!" Althea called. "Come join us."

The twelve soldiers, plus Thomas, organized themselves by military rank into one long line.

"March!" said the squire, and Althea grabbed the back of Rosemary's shift. Rosemary was just one of the audience now, wedged between her mother and Mrs. Bathsheba, the smith's wife.

"I notice that Mr. DiAngeli isn't marching." Mrs. Bathsheba sniffed over Rosemary's head.

"They needed only one extra," said Althea.

"He was probably a Tory. All Papists are Tories."

"He couldn't have been five years old when the war started," Althea said with some asperity.

"There'll be a problem with that family," Mrs. Bathsheba warned. "Mark my words."

The parade ended. The squire stood on the top step of the mill and read the Declaration of Independence out loud. Then the miller delivered the same address that he gave every year.

"Where's Philip?" said a loud whisper into Rosemary's ear: A-Two. "Have you seen Philip? Isn't he here?"

The miller ended his speech, and all the women began to unload food from the backs of their wagons. A-Two waited and waited for Philip to arrive. Finally, reluctantly, she cut into her special cake: a slice for her father, a slice for the squire, a slice for Mr. DiAngeli, even one for Benjie. But never, ever, a slice for Philip. "It tastes good," Rosemary said; she almost felt sorry for her sister. By midafternoon, when it was time to pack the wagon and go home, A-Two's face had become pale with waiting.

Once home, though—with Con and Colin and Rosemary doing all of her afternoon chores—A-Two's old determination returned. She sat before her sliver of a mirror, dampening her hair and rolling it around tiny sticks until she looked like a porcupine. When her hair was dry, she bound her new curls at the top of her head with a ribbon. For the rest of that day, she hardly moved her head. And that evening, when she followed her parents and Rosemary around to the back of the squire's house, she walked as smoothly as a water bug gliding across flat water. "Oh, my hair?" she said nonchalantly in response to Mrs. Small's compliment. "It's nothing. They call it '*à la grecque*.' "

The young men were setting lanterns around the edges of the squire's lawn—spots of light on the ground, brightness from the branches of trees. The young men, like A-Two and the older girls, were dressed in their best: clean breeches, clean shirts. Philip stood out like a flower in winter with his embroidered waistcoat and his breeches of periwinkle blue.

"Beautiful!" he called to A-Two. He flew across the lawn, leaving his fellows to finish the work. He grabbed A-Two's hands; he twirled her around. Her curls flew. "Tonight you are beautiful!"

"Oh, Philip!" A-Two trilled.

The fiddler, fifer, and drummer readied their instruments. The parents and younger children stepped off the lawn. Rosemary stood beside the refreshment table and watched. A-Two danced the first dance with Philip, and the second one as well. For the third reel, A-Two accepted an offer from Hammond, Benjie's cousin. Sometime during the fourth dance, Philip disappeared.

A-Two helped herself to punch. She laughed with Mrs. Olivia Proctor. She let Mrs. Di-Angeli fix her ribbon and curls. With a big smile, she turned back to the dancers. At first she waited expectantly, happily. She squinted into the uncertain light, prepared to laugh and tease at any invitation. But there was none.

A-Two's smile faded. Her spine, her shoulders, became rigid.

"There's a bench here," Rosemary said from behind her sister, from back in the trees. "You can sit down if you want."

A-Two's shoulders jerked. "I didn't see you," she said. But she sat anyway. In silence she and Rosemary watched. The older people were dancing now. The DiAngelis danced together; the squire danced with Mrs. Olivia Proctor; even bony Miss Nancy Proctor danced—with Thomas Small.

"She's so old," A-Two mused. "Don't you think Miss Nancy Proctor is awfully old?"

They watched the whole of the fifth dance. The sixth dance ended. The fiddler tuned up for the seventh. Rosemary felt a tug at her elbow. She turned to see Benjie in a high state of silent excitement. He pointed toward a dark, empty window. The second, upstairs, on the left.

Sometimes in the course of changing history, a lie is necessary. "Philip told me," said Puck, "that if the Regulator Reel started without him, I should let him know."

"What?" said A-Two. "Where is he?"

Rosemary didn't even have to ask A-Two to follow. They walked onto the lawn, through the merrymakers, and into the house. The mirror in the mirror room reflected back their outlines like movements of silver. Upstairs, Rosemary found the room that belonged to the second window on the left. Even before she put her hand on the latch she heard a voice: "Darling," said Philip. "Sweetheart. Love."

"Oh, Philip!" A-Two trilled, and she pushed the door open.

Inside the dark room Philip was nothing more than a coverlet-draped dark mound on a dark bed. The coverlet moved; a head popped out. "Whoops!" said Tillie.

Rosemary couldn't see much, but she heard Tillie laughing, Philip swearing, and then A-Two's feet pounding back down the stairs.

Puck's heart stopped. Rosemary reached to the floor and let her fingers grab the objects that were there.

Out on the lawn the dancers were concentrating on their steps—in, out, back, around. The squire laughed by the punch bowl. Beneath the light of a lantern, Althea admired Mrs. DiAngeli's baby.

"Well?" Benjie popped up from nowhere.

"Where's A-Two?"

"She ran out of the house like a hive of bees was after her!"

With a hurt that was only a fraction her own, that was mostly her sister's, Rosemary nodded. "Here," she said. "Take this."

"What is it?" asked Benjie. "A shoe?"

"We're going to the mill."

The party would continue for hours yet. Nobody would miss A-Two. Nobody would miss two children. On Independence Day night, people always disappeared into shadows. They invariably showed up the next morning, safe in their own, or others', beds.

There was little moon, much starlight, but Rosemary hardly needed to see to find her way. She led Benjie almost to the mill, to where the millstream ended its run. She stood very, very still. Before her the river was a flowing, turning, starlit gleam.

"Why did we come?" Benjie asked. "What are we supposed to do?"

"This," said Rosemary, and she held Philip's left shoe high, then threw it as far downstream as she was able. A moment later Philip's right shoe plunked into the water, too.

"Yes!" said Benjie. "I liked that!"

And Puck's magic was no more.

CHAPTER 7

Friends

After Independence Day, Colin's corn was as high as Rosemary's chin. Only the year before she had been small enough to hide in the corn, watching the green stalks sway above her in the breeze, listening to her mother and her sisters call. But this July, Rosemary was visible from the chin up. She imagined what she must look like to the birds: a brownish, pinkish, whitish bump amongst all that green; a bump sprouting a peculiar kind of corn silk, much too dark, much too long. The real corn silk was down around Rosemary's fingertips, pushing upward from the very tops of the baby corn ears, waiting for rain to bring down pollen like a blessing. It was rain that would make the corn kernels grow and grow until they were yellow and plump and juicy and delicious. It was rain that *must* come if Rosemary's family was to eat corn bread throughout the winter.

"Ro-sie!"

For a moment Rosemary thought of folding her knees and disappearing. But it was her mother who called, not A-Two.

"Ro-sie!"

With care, edging sideways between the cornstalks, Rosemary left the field. Althea was in the kitchen garden, harvesting the last of the spring peas, the early lettuce, the haricot beans. "We have more than enough for ourselves," Althea told her daughter. "I want you to take this basket to the DiAngelis."

"Yes, Mama."

"And this." Althea put a melon in the very center of the basket.

Thus burdened, Rosemary walked down the wagon path. She placed one foot in front of the other, exactly in the rut of a wagon wheel. She swung the basket from her right hand; she swung it from her left. Because of the melon, it was too heavy to hold comfortably in one hand. And yet the basket was too large to hold against her stomach. She stepped out of the wheel rut and tried a new experiment: balancing the basket on her head. At first she took little mincing steps, like A-Two wearing shoes. Then she kept her knees bent and her feet low and glided like a water strider across the dust. She was pleased with herself—gliding seemed to work. She took her balancing hand away from the basket and glided on until, for no good reason, the basket tumbled from her head and dropped peas, beans, lettuce, and melon onto the sun-hardened path.

Only the melon really suffered. Rosemary looked at the three jagged-edged sections and made a decision: She would take the melon with her and leave it outside the DiAngelis' door. If Mrs. DiAngeli seemed a sympathetic sort of person, Rosemary would explain and hand the melon over. After all, the melon was still good enough to eat. But if Mrs. DiAngeli proved to be anything like Mrs. Bathsheba, the smith's wife, then Rosemary would kick the melon pieces behind the woodpile and let them rot.

The basket back in her hands, she continued

on her way. She saw Benjie and his brothers fishing at the millpond. Rosemary lifted her basket to her head—keeping her balancing hand in place—and glided past them.

"Hey, Rosie!" said Frankie, the brother closest to Benjie in age.

Rosemary, too busy to talk, turned up the path to the schoolhouse. She hadn't visited the schoolhouse since the day the baby was born and Mr. DiAngeli was felled by the tree. When Rosemary reached the schoolhouse yard, she stopped to look around.

The DiAngelis' garden wasn't half the size of Althea's, and only the tomatoes seemed to be doing well. The DiAngelis had arrived too late in the growing season for their garden to yield much. But they had tidied up the yard and arranged the schoolhouse benches in a pattern of constant triangles against the wall. Rosemary moved closer, to see. Where the edges of the benches met the ground, somebody had planted sprouts of honeysuckle. In a year or so, the wall would be a mass of scent and flowers.

Rosemary smiled.

She heard movement inside the house. In a

moment she had hidden the pieces of melon in three different corners where bench met wall. The basket dangled from her hand. "How do you do?" Rosemary said as the door opened and Mrs. DiAngeli looked out.

"Very well," said Mrs. DiAngeli. "And you?"

"I'm very fine. I hope that Mr. DiAngeli is also well?"

"He's well enough to work a full day, thanks to the Lord—and your mother."

"Mama sent these." Rosemary held out the basket.

"How lovely." Mrs. DiAngeli smiled at Rosemary. And then she laughed. "How very, very lovely! Won't you come in, Rosie? Won't you have some tea with me?"

Rosemary didn't understand the laughter, but she was pleased by the invitation. Drinking tea was the ultimate in adult behavior. She began to step over the threshold. She stopped. "I'm awfully dirty," she admitted.

"Not at all," Mrs. DiAngeli said comfortably. "After your hot walk here, you deserve something nice."

Rosemary agreed. "Thank you," she said.

The inside of the schoolhouse looked the same as before, but different. Today it was filled with flowers. Masses of flowers in bowls and bottles and jars and cups. White daisies, yellow daisies, daisies as large as hands or as small as buttons. With the front door open, the daisies shining, and a little baby cooing from a nest of bedclothes on top of the bed, it was the nicest room that Rosemary had ever seen. "Oh!" she exclaimed.

"Do you like flowers?" asked Mrs. DiAngeli.

"Yes, ma'am." Rosemary was suddenly shy.

"Please," said Mrs. DiAngeli, "sit down."

Rosemary sat primly on the edge of a stool.

"I don't think you want hot tea," said Mrs. DiAngeli. "So let me give you some of my special mint tea. It has honey in it."

"All right," and Rosemary waited until she was handed a mug of cool, sweet tea. "It's warm weather we're having," she remarked, as politely as a lady come to call. She took her first sip. "My, how delicious!"

Again Mrs. DiAngeli laughed. Rosemary glanced up. Mrs. DiAngeli recomposed her face. "I'm not behaving very well, am I?" she

119

said. "Let me start over." She sat across from Rosemary, took her own mug in hand, and nodded gravely at her guest. "Very warm weather, indeed," she pronounced in a stately manner.

Rosemary felt her nose crinkle and her mouth curl upward. She bit her lip and looked deeply into her mug.

"We are, of course," Mrs. DiAngeli continued, as formally as before, "hoping for a spell of rain."

Rosemary snorted.

"It will benefit the crops," said Mrs. DiAngeli, "don't you think?"

Rosemary's snort became a full explosion: a blustering laugh. And then she and Mrs. DiAngeli were laughing together, bouncing and swaying on their stools. Tears popped from Rosemary's eyes into her tea. "How silly!" she cried.

"You—!" Mrs. DiAngeli gasped.

"No, you—!" Rosemary wheezed. And for just a moment she gathered all her laughter together, holding it in abeyance. Although her mouth was still smiling, her nose still running, she looked at Mrs. DiAngeli very, very seriously. She had never, ever laughed like this with an adult before. "You're so old—," she began to say, but her laughter broke forth. She bent her head down to wipe her face on the skirt of her shift.

Mrs. DiAngeli laughed and laughed, but even she had to stop to breathe. "I'm not *that* old," she protested.

"You're older than A-Two," Rosemary said. "And A-Two *never* laughs."

"Then something is wrong with A-Two," said Mrs. DiAngeli.

"No," responded Rosemary. "I think she was just born persnickety."

"That's possible, too. Don't you have another sister? Does she laugh?"

"That's Con." Rosemary considered all the difficulties of talking about Con. "She's different."

"So I hear. But does she laugh?"

Rosemary pictured Con in the forest, Con turning pages with her eyes, Con somehow talking to her friend. "She laughs," said Rosemary. "But I think she mostly laughs inside." She touched her chest.

"For some people," said Mrs. DiAngeli, "that's the very best kind of laughter."

"Maybe," said Rosemary. But she thought her own life would be silent and sad if she never laughed out loud.

"More tea?" Mrs. DiAngeli offered.

Rosemary accepted. She watched Mrs. DiAngeli stand and move; she observed the plumpness of the woman's hand; she studied the sweetness of the woman's face. "How old are you?" she suddenly asked. It was a rude question, but she couldn't help herself.

"I'm nineteen and a half," Mrs. DiAngeli replied promptly, not at all offended.

Rosemary sighed with relief. "You're hardly older than Con. And I thought you were a lady!"

"Well, I am—in a way. I have a husband, and a baby, and a house, and a garden."

"Not a very good garden," said Rosemary.

"No," Mrs. DiAngeli admitted.

"Maybe I could help you with your garden."

"I would like that. I would like that *very* much."

Rosemary felt greatly contented. And then she remembered: "I have something more for you. It's outside." She set her mug on the table and ran out of the house. Mrs. DiAngeli followed.

"It's here," said Rosemary. "And here . . . and here." From their dark little corners she pulled each of the separate pieces of melon. While Mrs. DiAngeli watched, she fitted them back together to make a whole. "There!"

"A melon," said Mrs. DiAngeli. "For me?"

"I was walking," said Rosemary, and she let her hands holding the melon loosen, so that the pieces once again shifted apart. "And *boom!*"

They laughed until Mrs. DiAngeli sighed with pleasure. "You'll come again, won't you, Rosie?" she said. "You'll come again soon?"

"I'll come tomorrow," Rosemary promised. "Or as soon as Mama will let me."

"I'll be waiting," said Mrs. DiAngeli.

Walking down the path, back to the mill, Rosemary swung the lightened basket from her hand. When she saw Benjie and his brothers still fishing, she lifted her other hand to wave. "I got a two-chipper, Rosie!" Frankie called. "A *big* two-chipper. Come and see!"

Rosemary shook her head, surprising even herself. Only yesterday she would have rushed to the millpond to try her own luck. But today she hardly even imagined the taste of white sugar; she still had the real taste of honey and mint in her mouth.

"Watch Rosie mosey, she thinks she's a posy. Instead she's a great big *stink*!" Frankie shouted.

Rosemary ignored the jibe. Instead, she put one foot in front of the other, the next foot up forward again, and so swayed home along the wagon path. It was as she walked that the rain came, at first small drops, and then big, satisfying drops that hit the earth with a splatter of dust. Rosemary put the basket over her head upside down and—with the handle bouncing against her chin—watched her shift and feet get increasingly wet. When she had passed the Smalls' turnoff and was almost at her own family's fields, she made a sudden left turn and disappeared into the forest.

Inside the forest there was no rain. There was

only the sound of rain, high above, and an occasional drip downward from tulip poplar leaf to oak leaf to dogwood leaf to a fern upon the ground. Rosemary left the basket almost within sight of the wagon path and went searching for Con.

She found her sister with the pigs in the very thickest part of the forest, on the leeward side of a bluff. She stopped, waiting, until the big sows had adjusted to her presence, until Con smiled at her.

"Hello, Rosie."

"I thought I'd come talk to you."

"All right," said Con.

Rosemary sat down beside her sister. "I think I made a friend today."

"Good!" Con encouraged.

"Mrs. DiAngeli. We laughed. We laughed a lot. We hardly had to say anything to make the other laugh."

"That sounds like a friend," Con agreed.

Rosemary picked up a fallen hickory leaf. Methodically she began to pull leaflet after leaflet from the stem. "We talked about you," she said.

"Oh?"

"I just said that you laugh," Rosemary hastened to explain. "You do, don't you? With the Indian?"

"Yes."

Rosemary looked sideways at her sister. "Is that why the Indian is your friend?"

"Partly," Con mused. "But it's more than that. He's as different from his people as I am from mine; that's why he left his tribe, a long time ago. But then he found me. And I finally found somebody with whom I can feel alike. I don't have to explain to him; I don't have to hide. I don't always have to be thinking about who he is or what I am. Instead, when I'm with him I can think about the really important things—like how deep is the sky."

"Oh!" Rosemary had no other reply. Con had never spoken to her like this before. Yesterday, Rosemary had been nothing more than a little sister; today, Con was treating her almost as an equal. Contradictorily, Rosemary felt humbled. "Maybe I can be like you, too," she ventured, "some."

"It's too soon to tell yet," said Con, and she

126

changed the subject. "Do you want me to tell you a story? I don't think I can read one to you, not now; with the rain, Papa will soon be inside."

"No," Rosemary declined, "thank you. I'll just think." And with her sister warm against her side, Rosemary snuggled back against the fallen log and thought. She thought about the rain that was falling harder now, breaking through the leaf canopy overhead. She thought about the sky above the clouds, which she had always assumed went on into blue forever, but maybe it didn't. She thought about raindrops on the river, and raindrops on the river rocks, and little birds pressed against tree trunks just as she was pressed against this log, to stay dry. And she thought about what it would be like to have nobody in the whole world with whom to share her thoughts, and she suddenly felt very, very lonely.

"A rain without thunder," Con mused. "That's unusual for this time of year."

"Yes," said Rosemary. "Yes, it is." And almost faster than she could think, she leaned over and kissed her sister's cheek. "I have to go get my basket. I left it beside the road. I'll see you again at home."

"Yes," said Con, and she put a finger on top of Rosemary's kiss.

Rosemary ran back through the forest as if the pigs were after her, although she knew they weren't. The forest was as wet as soup now, as green as a firefly's bottom. She grabbed her basket, now as damp as she, and emerged onto a road that was awash with rain and slick with red mud. She ran home spattering mud upward, onto her shift, and when she pulled the door open she heard voices, everybody's voices: her father's, her mother's, A-Two's.

"A good, steady rain!" That was Colin.

"You remembered the coffee. Thank you." That was Althea.

"It's a letter from Caroline!" That was A-Two.

Colin, like Rosemary, was wet and mud-spattered and cheerful. He sat beside the table, rubbing his head with a towel. "Hey, Rosie!" he said.

Althea looked up from the bags and sacks that she was opening. She motioned with her head toward the linen chest. "You need a towel, too."

A-Two stood before the half-open back door, a sheet of paper held in the rainwater light. If she hadn't been reading, she would have been crying: Her face was that long and that sad.

"Are all the DiAngelis well?" Althea asked.

"I think so," said Rosemary. She stared at A-Two.

Althea turned. "What is it, A-Two? Is something wrong? What does Caroline write?"

"She's not coming home!" A-Two wailed. "She's not coming home until September!"

"Is she ill?" Althea was worried. "Is her mother ill?"

"They're having a wonderful time!"

Colin chuckled. "I heard about that young miss's wonderful time at the mill today. The squire had a letter, too. It seems that Caroline has found herself a young man. A harmless young man, from what I could tell—he writes for a paper back in New Bern. But the squire was blustering and puffing. Jeffersonian politics, that's the young man's interest. Of course, the squire has always favored Hamilton—thinks that since he's Washington's protégé, he can't do anything wrong. Why, we were talking about the national debt, and . . ."

Rosemary stopped listening to her father. Her mother, she noticed, had her ears turned toward Colin but her eyes turned toward A-Two.

A-Two sniffled—a long, loud sound. She dropped her letter and fled up the ladder-stairs to the attic room. Rosemary got to the letter in an instant. For a moment she considered reading it, but she knew that her mother was watching. Instead, she picked up the letter by a corner and carried it, dangling, up the ladder-stairs.

A-Two lay on her back on her pallet, staring up at the rafters. Her eyes were wide with suffering. Rosemary dropped the letter onto her sister's stomach; it slid off, returning to the floor.

"Did he notice her because of the gown?" Rosemary asked.

A-Two's mouth moved, but no sound came out.

Rosemary sat down on the edge of A-Two's

pallet. "It was awfully pretty," Rosemary remarked. "But she still is awfully fat."

"It's not fair!" A-Two finally spoke.

"What? That she's fat?"

"That she's fat, and rich, and that she's in New Bern having a wonderful time!"

"It's not so awful here," said Rosemary.

"She's going to parties, and shopping with her mother. She's visiting friends. She has a beau!"

"You have a beau," Rosemary encouraged, thinking of Thomas Small. "Well, maybe. Well, maybe not."

And to Rosemary's chagrin, A-Two—her angry, feisty, persnickety sister—turned onto her stomach and cried.

CHAPTER 8

Art

Christmas was months away, almost half a year away, but Rosemary and Mrs. DiAngeli were making candy. Rosemary had pulled the slender gingerroots from the forest floor; Mrs. DiAngeli had volunteered her store of brown sugar. Now they were working together in the DiAngelis' house. Mrs. DiAngeli was stirring the pot of boiled sugar water, trying to make it cool faster. Rosemary had cleaned a long line of supple ginger sticks, which now marched down one whole side of the table.

". . . and then," said Rosemary, "there are the spiders."

"I like spiders, too," said Mrs. DiAngeli.

"The big yellow ones," said Rosemary, "with the orange and white legs."

"Those great, hairy wolf spiders," said Mrs. DiAngeli, "as big as baby Flavio's hand."

"The little spiders," said Rosemary, "with the hard, triangular shells on their backs."

"The underwater fishing spiders."

"Underwater?"

"You must have seen one—about three inches long with its legs stretched out—walking on top of the water. They creep below the surface, to hunt tadpoles and small fish."

"Ooh!" said Rosemary.

"You'll see one. Just sit beside the river sometime, where the stream isn't too fast . . . I think the syrup is cool enough now." Mrs. Di-Angeli poured the sugar water into a jug. She and Rosemary arranged the gingerroots in the jug as though they were flower stems. "There. Now we just have to let it sit and wait until Christmas."

"Christmas!" Rosemary sighed. She wandered around the house while Mrs. DiAngeli cleaned and put away the dishes they had dirtied. Baby Flavio, in his nest on top of the bed, smiled. "Look!" Rosemary called, and Mrs. DiAngeli came running. "He smiled at me!"

Mrs. DiAngeli scooped her baby into her arms and kissed him. "He does that now. He's growing so fast!"

"He knows me," said Rosemary, pleased. "He knows me!"

"Of course he does. He knows you, and Miss Nancy Proctor from the mill. And Mrs. Olivia Proctor sometimes comes by, although she's usually busy with her own baby. We don't often see the smith's children, which surprises me. There are so many of them!"

"Too many," said Rosemary. "You wouldn't want them to visit."

"I thought you and Benjie were friends."

"Benjie's a nuisance."

"Nuisances have a way of becoming husbands. That happened to me."

Rosemary grimaced.

Mrs. DiAngeli smiled. "I have something to show you," she said. "I took it out for Baby to see, and then I kept it out for you."

She shifted the baby onto her hip, reached for a box on a shelf, and then set the box down on the bed beside Rosemary. "Open it."

But first Rosemary touched the box. It was a carved box, unlike any she had ever seen before. The wood was red and smooth, and beneath her fingers it turned into flowers and fishes and birds, each figure separate, each one somehow melting into the next. "Oh!"

"I made the box. Now, open it."

"You made this?"

"What you will find inside, my great, great, eleven-times-great-grandmother made."

Very carefully, Rosemary pushed open the lid. What was inside also looked carved—but it wasn't, because it was made of metal. It was a strange, flat, black metal jug. Rosemary lifted it into her hands. "It's so . . ."

"Ugly?" said Mrs. DiAngeli. "Beautiful?"

"Both," said Rosemary. She turned the jug over and over, and each time she turned it, she saw something different: At first glance the jug was a graceful bird, a long-necked bird with the tip of its beak touching its breast; but then the tail of the bird was a flower, an open trumpet flower; and on the back, between the half-open wings, was a face, a fierce and grimacing face

135

with a huge, open mouth; underneath the bird, what should have been feet were horns, the horns of a goat-faced man. "What is it?"

"It's a lamp. A little oil lamp. You put the wick down into the flower, and then you pour oil into the big hole—"

"The mouth," Rosemary corrected.

"The mouth. And then you carry it by the swan's neck."

"The swan?"

"The bird."

"I thought it was a goose."

"No, in Italy, where my many-great-grand-mother lived, there were swans."

"Oh," said Rosemary, and she ran her fingers over the swan's head and beak. "Benjie's pa never makes anything like this."

"No. It takes a different skill. It's made of bronze. My many-great-grandmother first shaped the figures out of wax. Then she put clay all around, melted out the wax, and poured bronze into the mold. It's very different from making horseshoes and plows."

"I don't know if I like it," said Rosemary. "I mean, I do like it. But I don't."

Mrs. DiAngeli took the lamp into her own hands. "That's because it means so much," she said. "I feel the same way. This is beauty and fear and anger—and whatever life is. It's all here, in this one little lamp. My grandmother was an artist."

An artist. Rosemary had heard that word before; now she knew what it meant.

"So I take it out," said Mrs. DiAngeli, "now and again. And I feel it with my fingers, and I hold it, and I look at it, and I think about what my many-great-grandmother was trying to say. And what she did say. And then I realize that the world is really much bigger than what I know."

Rosemary was no longer sure that she understood. She touched the box again. "You made the box," she said.

"When I was young. When my mother first gave me the lamp. It was her special gift to me. She had some skill of the hands; I had more. I carved this box just after my sixteenth birthday. A year later I married Flavio, and I didn't carve much after that."

"But can you?" asked Rosemary. "Can you still do this?" She kept her hand on the box.

"I suppose so. I just need some good hardwood. I have the knife."

"You could make more boxes," said Rosemary. "You could make toys. You could make a doll for baby Flavio!"

"All I really need is the wood," Mrs. DiAngeli said again, almost wistfully.

"There's a tree out back," said Rosemary. "It fell last year. It's walnut."

She would never have guessed that it would take so much thought to choose a piece of wood. In Rosemary's opinion, almost every branch of the fallen tree was just fine. But Mrs. DiAngeli felt and stroked and tested the limbs with her hands; she brought her face as close as she could and peered.

"Look, Rosie," she said. "Right here. Do you see? It's almost a face already." And Rosemary, putting her eyes right up to the length of tree limb, saw nothing but bark.

"This will do," said Mrs. DiAngeli. "And this one, too. We'll try them both. They'll be very different faces."

Rosemary obediently chopped off the branch

sections with Mr. DiAngeli's smallest ax. She followed as Mrs. DiAngeli carried one of the sections back inside, still feeling it with her hands. "Ah!" Mrs. DiAngeli said. "Yes! Oh, of course." Rosemary had no idea what she was talking about.

But when Mrs. DiAngeli sat down at the table with her special little knife and began to carve, Rosemary began to see. What had been a knob was the back of a head. What had been a twig stump was the very tip of a tiny nose. She was watching a carving, but it was more like watching an unwrapping. The knife skimmed, it curved, and from underneath its blade a face emerged.

"It's a baby!" said Rosemary.

"It's a little girl, I think," said Mrs. DiAngeli. "Not a boy."

"Yes." There was something about the nose, about the cheekbones that made Rosemary certain: This doll was a girl. "She's beautiful!" Rosemary sighed.

"She *is* pretty," said Mrs. DiAngeli.

"I'll make her a gown," said Rosemary.

"A stuffed body, then, for hugging." Mrs. Di-Angeli was thinking out loud. "I'll carve her some little hands and some little feet."

When Mr. DiAngeli came home, baby Flavio was clean and dry and sleeping in his nest. Rosemary was working with a piece of muslin, making careful stitches down the back of a tiny body and tiny legs and arms. Mrs. DiAngeli sat at the table staring at the second piece of wood.

"Maria?" said Mr. DiAngeli.

Mrs. DiAngeli frowned at her husband as though he weren't there. Rosemary, less engrossed in her stitches than Mrs. DiAngeli was in her wood, stared.

"Maria?" Mr. DiAngeli said again. He looked normal, as far as Rosemary could tell. She hadn't seen him since Independence Day, and before that she hadn't seen him since the bloody day when baby Flavio was born. She had only Benjie's report, and the reports of other neighbors, that he sometimes fell onto the ground and threw his arms around. He was a dark-haired, handsome, and somewhat tired-looking young man; he didn't appear to be the kind of person who enjoyed surprising other people by doing sudden and unexpected things.

"Isn't it time for supper?" said Mr. DiAngeli.

"Supper!" Rosemary put down her needle. "Mama will be wondering!"

"Supper." And Mrs. DiAngeli's eyes widened. "Oh, my! Flavio, I'd forgotten!"

Mr. DiAngeli laughed. "Don't go yet, Rosie. Show me what you've been making."

Rosemary held out the little sewn body and the little muslin sausages of arms and legs. She had been a bit worried for Mrs. DiAngeli until that laugh. She liked Mr. DiAngeli's laugh. It made him look less tired.

"It's a doll," said Mrs. DiAngeli, and Mr. DiAngeli picked up from the table a tiny hand curved into a loose fist, and a tiny foot caught when the toes were still wriggling.

"I must go," said Rosemary. "Really, I must." She slipped through the doorway, turning around only once, to see Mr. and Mrs. DiAngeli smiling at each other.

"No supper," said Mrs. DiAngeli.

"No supper," Mr. DiAngeli repeated, and he laughed again.

Rosemary felt like laughing herself as she ran home—even though it was now very late. The roadside chicory blossoms were closed up tight. All the birdcalls were evening calls: the liquid warble of the wood thrush, the repeated command from the towhee that Rosemary go home and drink her tea-ea-ea.

She raced into her front yard and ran through the open front doorway. "Mama!" she yelled. "Mama!"

Althea and the others looked up from the supper table. Colin, for once, was stern.

"I made a doll!" Rosemary skidded to a stop against the back of her mother's chair. "I made a doll!"

"Fine," said her father, "fine. But why are you so late?"

"Because," said Rosemary. "Because art is important."

After supper, after feeding the chickens, Rosemary attached herself to A-Two. She climbed the ladder-stairs with her forehead almost touching A-Two's heels. She peered into the corner where A-Two kept her belongings.

When A-Two picked up a large, pale bundle, Rosemary was cheered.

"What do you think you are?" A-Two snapped. "A puppy?"

"I'll help," Rosemary volunteered. "I'll get the scissors!"

"Don't you dare *touch* my scissors," said A-Two.

Rosemary could have managed a tart reply, but instead she stood aside and let her more difficult sister descend the ladder-stairs alone. When A-Two began to unfold her bundle on top of the table, Rosemary was instantly beside her.

"What?" snapped A-Two.

"Nothing," said Rosemary, and she watched as the fine, blue-sprigged muslin—the same fabric that had made Caroline almost pretty—unfolded in pieces. "You've already cut it!"

"Some of it."

"Will it look like Caroline's?"

"Will you stop asking questions!"

Rosemary fell silent.

A-Two picked up one long piece and held it just below her bosom. "Hmmm," she muttered.

Rosemary sat down on a stool and waited. She waited until the flat pieces and the strange shapes began to meet in the roundness of a long, slender, high-busted gown.

"If I pin this here . . ." A-Two looked around. "Pin this on my back. Can you see where?"

Rosemary could easily see where. She had been watching the making of the gown for more than an hour. She pinned a piece of blue-sprigged bodice onto the back of A-Two's stays. "The waist is even higher than Caroline's," she ventured.

"Hmmm," said A-Two, but it wasn't an unfriendly sound.

Rosemary took hope. "It'll be pretty."

"It will be different," A-Two replied. "Do you see what I'm doing?"

Rosemary wasn't sure what she was supposed to see.

"I'm changing the whole shape of a formal gown. Nobody's done this yet, I'm sure. It's all my own idea." And then, with a spark of the real A-Two: "And it's going to make everybody, *everybody* notice me!"

"Your bosom's going to show."

"I intend it to."

Now that she and her sister were almost talking together, Rosemary thought that it might be time. She picked up a scrap of the sprigged muslin and said, "There's cloth left over."

"I'll use it," said A-Two. "Ruffles or something. Baste this sleeve."

Rosemary basted the sleeve. "If you have any little scraps," she said offhandedly, "enough for a doll's gown, would you give them to me?"

"I might," said A-Two. "Stand back and look at the hem. What do you think?"

Rosemary did not think the hem needed ruffles, but that was not what she said. "It will just touch your toes once it's sewn."

"Good." A-Two was satisfied.

"The scraps?" said Rosemary.

Later, when it was night and most of the family was in bed, Rosemary lay on her pallet and looked into the dark. She could almost—but not quite—see her box where it was stuck into the wall. Inside the box—held within its plain, sturdy sides—there were now four scraps of cloth. After all the hours Rosemary had spent

145

as a seamstress's maid, A-Two had been generous. With her mind, with her memory, Rosemary touched that fine fabric, finer than any garment her mother or sisters now owned, finer than anything ordinary people wore. "Miranda," she whispered. She would call the baby doll Miranda; she would sew a gown for a princess.

The next morning, as soon as Althea let her go, Rosemary ran like the wind to the DiAngelis' house. The wrens called to her as she passed: *Here you are, then. Here you are, then.* A bluster of air, Rosemary blew in through the DiAngelis' front doorway. Mrs. DiAngeli was already working at the table. Miranda—her body, feet, and hands all attached—sat against a pitcher.

"Oh!" Rosemary exclaimed.

Mrs. DiAngeli glanced up and grinned. "And look at this," she said. She was sewing another little body, another pair of arms and legs. Watching her every stitch, with sleepy eyes, was another wooden head.

This doll was a boy, with whorled ears and a mouth just beginning to yawn. He didn't have as much wooden hair as Miranda had, but he was bigger. Rosemary thought rapidly. "Ferdinand," she said.

"Who?" said Mrs. DiAngeli.

"His name is Ferdinand," Rosemary explained. "Her name is Miranda."

"I thought," said Mrs. DiAngeli, "that we would give the little boy to Mrs. Olivia Proctor's baby."

"All right," said Rosemary, even though she was secretly disappointed. "I brought cloth for gowns. There's enough for two."

After Mrs. DiAngeli had touched and admired the cloth, Rosemary began making the gowns. She sewed with her tiniest stitches. She made little drawstrings for the necks and wrists; she sewed dainty ruffles onto the hems. She made one lovely little gown, and one gown that was nice but not quite so lovely. When she was finished, Mrs. DiAngeli had completed Ferdinand's body and limbs and was sewing him together.

"There!" said Rosemary.

"There!" said Mrs. DiAngeli.

"They are beautiful!" said Rosemary.

"They are," Mrs. DiAngeli agreed complacently. "Let's go visiting!"

Carrying doll Ferdinand and baby Flavio, they walked down the hill. The first person they saw to talk to was the miller. He stood outside his mill, stamping his feet and waving his arms. "Sometimes," he explained, "I get to sneezing, and I just have to come out here. Good morning, ma'am. How's Baby?"

"Thriving."

"And what's this?" The miller peered into Rosemary's arms. "Looks almost real, it does!"

"We made it," said Rosemary. "Well, I helped."

"We're taking it to Mrs. Olivia Proctor," said Mrs. DiAngeli. "As a gift."

"Oh, but won't she like that, though! You'll find them at the house. I think they're dyeing wool today."

Rosemary and Mrs. DiAngeli continued on their way. They found the miller's ladies behind the house, all gathered around a boiling pot, all staring fixedly into its depths. Mrs. Olivia Proctor's baby, almost old enough to walk, had pulled himself up against the edge of the porch;

he looked afraid to let go. Nobody noticed the visitors' arrival.

"More pokeweed, I think," said the miller's wife.

"Maybe a little," Mrs. Olivia Proctor agreed.

"This much, I think," said Miss Nancy Proctor, and the other two ladies nodded in unison.

Mrs. DiAngeli cleared her throat. "Hello," she said.

At the sound, Miss Nancy Proctor, startled, dropped a whole handful of twigs into the cauldron. The Proctor baby lost his grip and fell, screaming, onto the ground. Mrs. Olivia Proctor turned toward her baby. The miller's wife turned toward Mrs. DiAngeli. There was a general confusion of legs and arms and direction of movement over by the dye pot.

Rosemary, always a lady, managed not to laugh.

"I'm sorry!" Mrs. DiAngeli cried out. "Oh, I'm so sorry!"

"There's no harm done," the miller's wife said briskly. "Nancy?"

"No harm at all," Miss Nancy Proctor repeated. "Look—I think it will be just the right shade." And with the others, Rosemary and Mrs. DiAngeli stepped up to look into the red, red pot.

The Proctor baby stopped crying. "Look, Paulie!" Mrs. Olivia Proctor cooed. "Soon we'll have a pretty red gown for you."

Rosemary glanced at Mrs. DiAngeli. Mrs. DiAngeli nodded. "We have something for Paulie, too," said Rosemary. She held out the doll. "His name is Ferdinand."

Little Paulie regarded the doll with suspicion, but his mother was rapt. Her mouth fell partly open as she gazed. "It's beautiful!"

"Mrs. DiAngeli made it. I helped," said Rosemary.

"Why . . ." Mrs. Olivia Proctor put her baby back on the ground and steered him away from the fire with an experienced, unthinking toe. "It's . . . you *made* this?"

"Yes." Mrs. DiAngeli spoke shyly.

"Mother, look! Nancy!"

Rosemary put Ferdinand into Mrs. Olivia Proctor's hands.

"It's absolutely exquisite!" breathed Miss Nancy Proctor.

"I've never seen its like!" said the miller's wife.

"The little ear!" said Mrs. Olivia Proctor. "The little hand!"

"It couldn't be more perfect," the miller's wife pronounced.

Thin, bony Miss Nancy Proctor, whom no one would marry, looked up and smiled a smile of such genuine pleasure that Mrs. DiAngeli blushed.

"How did you do it?" asked Mrs. Olivia Proctor.

"It's just a skill that I have."

Paulie Proctor, less suspicious now, tugged at his mother's skirts. She bent to show him the doll.

"A cup of coffee?" suggested the miller's wife.

"Perhaps some tea?" said Mrs. Olivia Proctor.

It could have been a perfect morning, one of the best in Rosemary's memory, but at that moment the smith's wife came around the house. Mrs. Bathsheba followed exactly the same path that Rosemary and Mrs. DiAngeli had trodden. She held her youngest baby under one arm and a bundle of linsey-woolsey under the other. "I

151

brought my old gown," she announced. "Is the dye ready?"

"Mrs. Bathsheba," Mrs. Olivia Proctor said politely.

"Hello," said Mrs. DiAngeli.

"My heavens," said the miller's wife to Mrs. Bathsheba. "I forgot you were coming."

"The dye will be ready soon," said Miss Nancy Proctor.

"It's a very old gown. It needs freshening. Even red will do. What on earth is that?"

"A doll," Mrs. DiAngeli said meekly.

"A beautiful doll," Miss Nancy Proctor said stoutly.

"Paulie's doll," Mrs. Olivia Proctor said protectively.

"A devil's plaything, that's my opinion." Mrs. Bathsheba sniffed. "This doll is much, much too real. It's devil's work, it is."

"Perhaps I should go," said Mrs. DiAngeli.

"No, please, stay," said Mrs. Olivia Proctor.

"I think you *should* stay," Mrs. Bathsheba agreed. "I have news, and you should most certainly hear it."

"News?" said Mrs. DiAngeli.

Mrs. Bathsheba looked around to make sure of her audience. Only Paulie wasn't giving her his full attention. The woman lifted her head and opened her mouth wide. "I bring with me good news, blessed news—holy news, in fact. The Methodists are sending us a man of God, a circuit rider. He will come to us within the month. He will preach. He will give us the word of the Lord. He will baptize our babies."

"Oh!" Mrs. Olivia Proctor sounded pleased.

Mrs. DiAngeli seemed less pleased. "How nice," she said.

Mrs. Bathsheba looked directly at Mrs. Di-Angeli. "We need some godly influence amongst us," she said.

"Of course we do," said the miller's wife. "And we will be glad to have it. But shouldn't we get on with our work?"

The Proctor women forgot their offer of tea. Mrs. DiAngeli began to say goodbye. Mrs. Olivia Proctor took her hand and said, "Thank you. It was *so* good of you."

Mrs. DiAngeli didn't talk as she walked back around the miller's house. Rosemary didn't talk, either. But when they were a good distance away, almost back to the mill, Mrs. DiAngeli said, almost to herself, "But baby Flavio has already been baptized."

"How could that be?" Rosemary asked.

Mrs. DiAngeli looked down at her, sharing a confidence: "My husband baptized him. We Catholics can do that, you see."

"You don't need a preacher?"

"Not if we don't have one."

Rosemary considered that option. "I don't know much about preachers," she said. "I don't know if I've been baptized."

"Perhaps you should be," Mrs. DiAngeli said.

"Perhaps," said Rosemary. "Perhaps not."

"Why not?"

"Because . . . ," said Rosemary. But she didn't have a good reason that she could say out loud. She only had a feeling—more than a feeling, a conviction. She did not, she absolutely did not, like Mrs. Bathsheba, the smith's wife.

CHAPTER 9

Con

It was definitely the spider time of year; everywhere in the forest there were webs. Rosemary, in search of Con, couldn't help collecting spiderwebs on her face. She rarely saw the webs: The afternoon heat had dried them of droplets and there were no sunbeams beneath the tree canopy to make them shine. As Rosemary searched through the forest she repeatedly felt a tautness against her nose and forehead, a sound like a tiny explosion somewhere near her ear, and then the stickiness, the everywhere stickiness, of another spider mask.

Webs before her face, webs down by her feet: slopes and slides of filament, woven as tightly as skin. Webs like hammocks. Webs like walls. By the time Rosemary found Con, she trailed spiderwebs like veils. Even her eyelashes were gluey.

"Hello," said Rosemary.

"Hello," said Con.

"Are you alone?" Rosemary peered across the river.

"Yes."

"Does the Indian have a home? Where does he go when he's not thinking to you?"

"He's a wanderer," said Con. "Why did you find me?"

"Papa came home from the Smalls' at noontime. They've almost finished the spring wheat there. They may be at our farm as soon as this afternoon."

"All right."

"But I don't think we have to hurry. Mama didn't say we had to hurry."

Con nodded. She began to walk slowly, quietly alongside the river, moving her big arms and legs with practiced care. Behind her, Rosemary rustled and snapped and kicked pebbles into the water.

"Look," said Con. She squatted at the very

edge of the river, where the mottled sycamore roots were half in, half out of the water.

"What?" said Rosemary. "Where?"

"A fishing spider," Con whispered. "You wanted to see one."

Rosemary squatted, too. Only a moment later, what had been a small shadow at the edge of a riverbed rock became a reaching spider. A spider, catching a tiny fish.

"Ah," said Rosemary. Satisfied, she sat on a bench of sycamore root. Con sat beside her, their feet dangling in the water. They gazed into the middle of the river, where the big rocks turned the water into spray.

"How do you do it?" Rosemary asked. "How do you make a rock flip upside down?"

Con turned to look at her. Usually Con's gaze was as benevolent and mild as a midsummer breeze. Usually Con looked at everything the same way: spiders, trees, Rosemary. But right now her eyes were penetrating, serious. She stared at Rosemary as though Rosemary were something new, something unusual—a butterfly in winter. Rosemary squirmed.

Con nodded again, as if she had made up her

mind. "I look at the rock," she said, "and then I think."

"Do you tell the rock to flip over?"

"No. I ask it to."

Rosemary fixed her eyes on a rock. Very politely she asked the rock to flip over. Nothing happened. "I can't do it."

"Neither can A-Two."

"Why? Should I try harder?"

"You'll have to wait," said Con, "until the blood comes."

Rosemary was puzzled. "What does that mean?"

But Con wouldn't say anything further. "Don't tell Papa," she suddenly instructed. "Don't tell Papa what I said. Come, now. They'll be wanting us for the wheat."

They arrived home well before Colin. When Colin did appear—late that afternoon, hot and dusty, with little bits of wheat chaff sticking to his clothes—he was alone. "No harvest today," he said. "The others will come tomorrow, early. I don't think it will take any more than a day to cut our field. Then we'll move on to the squire's."

The next morning, just after dawn, Rosemary sat on the front stoop and watched the others arrive: Thomas Small and his father, with their long-handled scythes; Black Seth from the squire's, with one of the squire's scythes. They marched like early-morning warriors down the wagon path and stood before the house with their weapons at rest. "Is your papa ready?" Mr. Small asked.

Harvesting days were always part work, part holiday, but mostly work. First the visiting warriors and all the Westons—except for A-Two, who stayed in the house to cook—walked out to the field. Then each of the men, with great solemnity, pulled a head of spring wheat from its stalk. Together, individually, they rubbed the kernels out into the palms of their hands; they blew away the chaff; they chewed.

"It's ready," said Thomas. "I suppose."

"I don't think I like this idea of planting so late, Weston," said Mr. Small. "Of harvesting so late. 'Spring wheat,' you said, 'let's try it.'"

"It's a sorry head of grain," Seth agreed.

"Well," said Colin, "it was an experiment. A

new kind of wheat. Something different for us to learn from."

"Book farming," intoned Mr. Small, an edge of disapproval in his voice.

"It's only a small field," said Colin. "We each agreed to plant one small field."

The four men formed a line, two scythe-swings distant from each other. They began to walk. They stepped and cut, stepped and cut. Rosemary, Althea, and Con followed after, picking up the cut grain and bundling it into sheaves.

"It smells good," Rosemary told her mother. "Look!" She wove some stems into a wreath and set it on her head.

"Rosie," said her father.

Rosemary sighed and bent again to her work. As the morning wore on, she lost the urge to talk and to share. Eventually she lost her crown. She hardly cared. She was no longer Rosemary, a distinct person. She was part of a pulsing rhythm of bend and tie, bend and tie.

"Rosie," said Althea, "start gathering the sheaves."

Rosemary unkinked her back. She stood for a

160

minute and waited, letting the others move ahead. The four men worked almost in unison. Althea's strong fingers grabbed two handfuls of wheat and whipped a stray stalk around the bundle. Con appeared to move more slowly than her mother, but she had left almost twice as many bundles behind.

Rosemary stationed herself behind Con. Con's step was as silent as the scythes were noisy. Her face, whenever Rosemary saw it, was always placid, almost blank.

"Rosie," Colin called. "Bring us a bucket."

Rosemary jumped, sprung free. She ran for the house, leaping over a chicken. "Wheat," she told it. "When we do the threshing, you'll get your fill of wheat." She bounded up onto the porch and reached for a bucket.

"Who is it?" said A-Two. "What are you doing?" She poked her head through the back doorway.

"Getting water," said Rosemary.

"Do something for me first," said A-Two. "I have the bread baking and the pudding boiling. Stir the pudding."

Reluctantly, Rosemary went inside. The

161

house was hot, hotter than the sunniest summer day. The fireplace was lit with two fires. A-Two peered into the oven. Rosemary stood over the smaller fire, took hold of a wooden spoon, and stirred. She stirred resentfully at first, and then with increasing boredom. A-Two removed her loaves and laid them on the table. Rosemary turned her head to watch . . . and then forgot to stir because, on the little table against the wall, a page turned in a book.

"Stir!" said A-Two. "It will burn!" She grabbed the spoon from Rosemary's hand.

Rosemary didn't care: She left A-Two stirring and muttering; she walked over to the book table.

O Cicero, she silently read, *I have seen tempests when the scolding winds have rived the knotty oaks . . .*

The page gently turned.

. . . but never till tonight, never till now did I go through a tempest dropping fire . . .

Rosemary stepped back. She closed her eyes and tried to see the words that came next. She tried to feel the paper with her mind; she tried to touch the edges of the page with her thoughts. With all her power of will, she asked the page to turn. But when she opened her eyes, the book still lay flat.

She stepped forward and placed one finger inside the opened spine of the book. Like a feather, like a leaf—obeying not her will but Con's—the page finally lifted and turned, falling over her finger.

"Weren't you supposed to get water?" asked A-Two. "Won't they be waiting?"

"I'm going," said Rosemary. But she walked backward, away from the book. "A-Two," she said, "how does Con read?"

"Like you and I read," said A-Two.

"She doesn't," said Rosemary.

"Get the water!"

Normally, Rosemary would have sped from the porch to the well to the field, but on this day she moved slowly. She listened to her father's scolding without making excuses; she didn't even mention A-Two and the pudding. She just returned to her position at the very back of the field. And she watched her sister.

Calmly, rhythmically, Con continued to work. She stooped and she stepped. In movement and action she resembled everybody else. But she wasn't like anybody else. Not at all.

Colin called a halt. The harvesters gathered to eat the meal that A-Two had laid out beneath a tree at the edge of the field. Like Seth, Con sat apart from the others; like Seth, Con was habitually separate from any crowd. Rosemary sat down beside her sister. "I don't know where Rome is," she said shyly. "Where Cicero lives."

"Rome!" Mr. Small exclaimed. "Why would a little girl like you care about Rome?"

"Her friend, Mrs. DiAngeli, is Italian." A-Two was pert.

"Not Italian," Althea corrected. "American. But of Italian blood."

"They have tempests in Rome," said Rosemary. "And fire that falls from the sky."

"You have a most unusual little girl," Mr. Small commented.

"Rosie's always saying silly things." A-Two was pert again.

Rosemary squinted against the sunlight. A-Two had spoken to everybody, but she was watching Thomas Small. Thomas sat with his back against the tree, his face raised to the sky; he was making a point of ignoring A-Two.

The conversation turned away from Rome; the attention turned away from Rosemary. Rosemary, like Con, sat silent. But back in the field, for the rest of that afternoon—while the men finished cutting the wheat, while everybody stacked the sheaves up into shocks—Rosemary watched her oldest sister. She watched for clues, for answers. She watched in the hope of understanding what she had never really questioned before.

"Con's different," she told her mother.

"Yes," Althea agreed, but she was busy with her work.

"Why?" said Rosemary. "Why, Mama? What is it that *makes* Con so very different?"

"Oh, Rosie." Althea sighed. "Rosie . . ." But Mr. Small called for Althea's assistance then, and Althea left Rosemary's question unanswered.

The next morning, only Rosemary and her father walked to the squire's. They walked in the dark, the last, heavy shadows of night surrounding them like shawls. "Good morning, Weston, Rosie," said Mr. Small. Having met on the wagon path, they turned together up the squire's track.

The squire was in the best of moods, stomping around his spring wheat field, measuring stalk height, tasting grain. "Ha! Mr. Weston," he called jovially as the others neared. "Look what we got for your experiment!"

"I know," Colin said wearily.

" 'We should try a field each,' that's what you said. Spring wheat! We'll get four bushels less of spring wheat per field than we did of winter wheat. That's what I think."

"We three agreed to the experiment," Mr. Small reminded the squire.

"So we did," the squire said. "So we did. 'Agricultural reform. An example to the neighborhood.' Ha!" But his laugh wasn't unkind. "Shall we start? I can promise you a fine noon meal!"

Today the squire wore nothing but breeches

and a shirt. No shoes, no waistcoat—he looked as much as possible like the other men. He grabbed his scythe and, with Colin and Mr. Small, settled himself into a pattern of stepping and cutting. Seth, Thomas, and Rosemary stood behind, waiting for the first stalks of wheat to fall.

"The squire's cheerful," Thomas remarked to Seth.

"He loves harvest, any harvest," Seth answered. And the two swung into their pattern: bundle and bind.

Rosemary lagged. She didn't have a real job today. She was supposed to pick up any stalks of wheat that Seth and Thomas missed; she was supposed to run errands. She watched the men bending to their labors, and she wondered if they thought about anything other than the dust and the sun and the feel of scythe or wheat in their hands.

"Rosie!"

Her first errand: She ran to the house in search of Tillie and a length of clean cloth with which to bind the squire's cut finger. She found Tillie weeping in the kitchen. Tillie wept as she searched for the bandages; she wept as she cut a piece to the right length.

"Can't you stop crying?" Rosemary asked.

"Not with Master Philip gone," Tillie sobbed.

Rosemary sped back to the field. She held the bandage patiently while the squire spit on his finger and then rubbed it dry on his shirt. "Is Philip really gone?"

"That rascal!" the squire said fondly. "A good day of hard work coming up, and he decides that he has to go—right away—back to Virginia. I expect he'll visit us again sometime."

The other men hadn't stopped. The squire blended himself back into their rhythm. For hours—for a time that lasted forever; for a time that, in its sameness, lasted only a moment— the harvesters worked. And then Tillie was ringing her bell; the men were straightening their backs. Rosemary had a new place to work: the kitchen.

In the kitchen, Tillie still mourned. "Master Philip was so sweet," she grieved. "So sweet!"

As sweet as a beesting, Rosemary thought. She took the plate that Tillie prepared and carried it outside. Seth sat all by himself on the kitchen stoop. Rosemary paused. She narrowed her eyes and observed. In his own way, Seth was as different as Con. "Are you lonely?" she asked, and she handed him the plate.

Seth looked up at her. He blinked, surprised. "Always," he said.

"Rosie!" Tillie called.

Inside, the other men all sat together around the big kitchen table. "Your son's a fine farmer, Small," the squire was saying. "It's been good this summer, having him with me. He's almost earned that heifer now."

"She's a nice beast," Mr. Small replied. "A fine little cow."

"And quiet," the squire commented. "Have you noticed? She doesn't low as much as the others do. She has a thoughtful look on her face."

The men all laughed. But Rosemary, cutting cake at the sideboard, looked up and toward the barn. She closed her eyes and thought hard. This time she didn't try to see, she tried to hear: a breath, a heartbeat, a shuffling hoof . . .

"Cake!" said Tillie. "Cut the cake! Are you daft?"

The sun was still high when Rosemary and her father walked home along the wagon path. The summer's second hatching of swallowtail butterflies, yellow and black, midnight blue and orange, crossed the path before them.

"Papa," said Rosemary, "why is it that Con can do the things she does?"

"Con works hard," Colin replied easily. "She's a good worker. She's handy with animals."

"No," said Rosemary. "That's not what I mean. I mean, why is it that she can do the *special* things she does?"

Colin didn't answer.

"Nobody else can do what Con does," Rosemary pursued, "except maybe Mama. Mama can do things, too. Why?"

"I don't know," Colin finally replied. "And I don't think your mother knows, either. It's a mystery, something that we weren't meant to know. But Rosie . . ." He stopped walking; he turned so that Rosemary couldn't help meeting his eyes. Colin's face was very serious. "I am certain—without a doubt—that your mother and Con *shouldn't* do those things. Not often. They know, as I know, that it would be dangerous for them if other people found out."

"Why? Who would hurt them?"

"And dangerous for the rest of us as well."

"No!"

"Believe me, Rosie. I'm asking you—no, I'm telling you—to believe me."

"All right," said Rosemary. She was surrounded by her father's eyes; she couldn't do anything but agree.

"We won't speak of such things again."

"No," Rosemary sighed.

Colin turned back to the road. Rosemary, now silent, continued walking beside him. She walked through the little flock of butterflies without reaching out to touch one. The world, somehow, had less color now.

At home, A-Two sat on the front stoop, picking through a bowl of berries. "Blackberries for supper," she called out, "and blackberry wine later on."

"Where's your mother?" Colin asked.

"In the springhouse."

Colin went around to the back of the house to wash up.

Rosemary stepped up and over A-Two. A-Two grabbed the hem of Rosemary's shift. "Tell me," A-Two said, and her voice was eager, "did you talk to Thomas? Did he mention me?"

CHAPTER 10

Evil

On the hottest day of summer, the very hottest, the traveling preacher arrived at the mill. He was a tall, imposing man on a spotted gray-and-white horse. Rosemary, who was fishing at the millpond, was one of the first to see him. Benjie and his brothers and sisters were the other people who were first. They were all sitting around the millpond: the little ones quarreling when their lines crossed, the middle ones shouting insults at each other, Rosemary and Benjie somnolent and dreaming.

The Bathsheba children were fishing for sugar chips, but Rosemary was going to give her catch to Mrs. DiAngeli. Right now, she hoped, Mrs. DiAngeli was carving. Benjie, across the millpond, had a little wooden fish in his pocket:

a perfect, leaping fish with a curved tail. The twins, Mary and Elizabeth, were caressing tiny carved lady dolls. Even Wash and Laffer, Rosemary's least favorite of that family, had funny bobbers to attach to their fishing lines: little wooden apples with worms at the top. When Rosemary had first seen those worms, with their narrow bodies curved up and down to make a loop for a horsehair line, she had been taken by a desire that was almost burning.

"I want to make something special for you," Mrs. DiAngeli had said. "Something very special. It will take time."

And so Rosemary, to give her friend time to carve, was fishing at the millpond with eight of the smith's children: Benjie, Frankie, Laffer, Martha, Wash, the twins, and little Ruth. It was Laffer who first heard the rider. Nobody was having any luck: The fish, like the children, probably found the afternoon too hot for movement. Laffer had turned away from the millpond, away from his floating apple, to stare morosely up the wagon path. Laffer never smiled.

"Listen!" he said.

Rosemary raised her head. She heard the sound of weary hooves.

"Is it Pa?" asked Martha, with some fear.

"It's a stranger!" said Frankie, and as one, the group was up on its feet and running. Rosemary, with Benjie, got to the preacher first.

"Hello," said Benjie.

"Are you wanting somebody?" asked Frankie. And then he added, "Sir."

Rosemary chose to stay silent. The preacher wore spurs, which she had seen only Philip Chalmers use before. He wore a long, mud-stained coat and an old black hat. Beneath that hat, his hair somehow stood straight out from his head. Rosemary put her hand on the gelding's soft nose. Unlike its master, the horse looked hot and tired.

"Bathsheba," said the preacher. "I am here to answer the call of sinners, to lead them away from evil and unto the Lord! Take me to Mrs. Bathsheba."

"That's Mama," Martha whispered.

"I'm Benjamin Bathsheba," said Benjie. "I can take you to my mother."

Eight smith's children and one Rosemary:

They made an escort of nine. Benjie led the way. Rosemary jostled with the others down the narrow path to the smith's place. The fire was out in the workshop. The house was unusually quiet, with only one baby crying.

"I'll hold your horse, sir," said Benjie, and the preacher dismounted. Rosemary looked straight upward: The preacher was even taller than Con. The smallest children, grouped so closely together that they might have been pasted, followed him to their front door.

"Go see if Mama is out back," Benjie told Laffer. "Frankie, find Pa." Benjie looked down at the reins in his hand.

"Tie up the horse," Rosemary told Benjie. "We should be in there, too."

She and Benjie reached the front doorway just as Mrs. Bathsheba walked in through the back. "Reverend!" Mrs. Bathsheba beamed. She promptly put the crying baby into Martha's arms. The youngest infant still slept. "Sit down, sir! Sit down!"

"Thank you, ma'am." The preacher sat.

"Benjie, get your father. Laffer, get the dandelion wine. You do drink, sir?"

"Never," said the preacher.

"Oh." Mrs. Bathsheba's effusiveness was stopped short for a moment. "Tea, then. Hot tea? Cold?"

"A glass of plain, cool water would suit me," the preacher replied.

"Laffer, bring water!"

Rosemary had never before seen Mrs. Bathsheba smile so much. She smiled with her lips parted, she smiled with her lips closed. She smiled with her head tipped to one side. "Reverend!" she said. "We are so grateful for your coming!"

"In the fields of the Lord," the preacher replied, "there are many weeds. I have come to pull them out."

Benjie wrinkled up his face; he glanced at Rosemary. She shrugged.

"We are blessed by your arrival," Mrs. Bathsheba gushed.

"The way of the Lord is clear," said the preacher. "Will I sleep here tonight?"

Later, out in the yard, Benjie and Rosemary unsaddled and rubbed the weary spotted horse.

"If he sleeps in the big bed," Benjie whispered, "and Mama and Pa sleep in our bed, then Frankie, Laffer, and I will have to sleep outside. What if it rains?"

"Your mama likes him," Rosemary whispered back. There was a yard, a stoop, a wall, and nine children between them and the preacher; but still, she whispered, too. "I imagine he will stay for a long time."

"He talks with too many words."

"He looks as mad as King Lear."

"King who? Is he in the Bible?"

"No. He's in another book." Rosemary stopped rubbing the horse. She took a step backward. " 'A knave, a rascal, a base, proud, shallow, beggarly, three-suited, hundred-pound, filthy worsted-stocking knave,' " she recited.

"No!" Benjie was entranced. "Where did you learn that?"

"There's more," said Rosemary, and she recited again: " 'A lily-livered, action-taking, whoreson, glass-gazing, superserviceable, finical rogue.' "

"That's fine!" Benjie breathed. "What does *whoreson* mean?"

"I don't know."

"It sounds bad," Benjie reflected. "Bad enough for Pa to whip me." He grinned.

"I'll wager you anything," Rosemary said, "that the preacher wears stockings made of worsted wool—like a knave!"

Benjie gulped air so that he wouldn't laugh out loud. "I'll find out," he said. "I promise you, I'll find out!"

The next morning Benjie showed up at the Weston farm for breakfast. "Good morning, ma'am," he said to Althea. "My mama sent me. She's sending me to all the farms this side of the mill. There's to be a baptizing this noon, at the millpond. My mama says that all sinners are invited."

"Sinners?" said Althea.

"I think Mama means anybody who hasn't been baptized. There are ten of us at our house."

"I see," said Althea.

Benjie took another slice of ham. "We have the preacher living with us right now," he continued. "In fact, this morning I saw that he wears stockings made of worsted wool."

"Ha!" Rosemary exploded.

"Rosie!" Althea chided.

When Benjie left for the next farm and his next breakfast, Althea stood on the stoop and watched him walk away. "It's going to be another hot day," she said. "A horribly hot day. Listen—the birds have already stopped singing."

"Are we going, Mama?" Rosemary asked casually. "To the mill?"

"Ohhh." Althea hung on to that word until it turned into a sigh. "Let me talk to your father."

"*I'm* not going," said A-Two from the cooler recesses of the house. "Just a lot of children— that's all it will be."

"Have you been baptized?" Rosemary asked her sister with interest.

"I'm a God-fearing woman," A-Two answered primly. "That's all that matters."

"Girls!" Althea interceded wearily. "Rosie, you clean the dishes." And with that she stepped down from the stoop and went to look for Colin in the cornfield.

Rosemary cleaned the dishes with a speed

that was absolutely foreign to the heat of the day. When she was done, she tore out of the house and into the front yard. She saw her mother and her father, deep in the cornfield, talking very earnestly, visible only from their noses up. Rosemary, like her parents, burrowed into the corn. When she was surrounded by nothing but green, she stopped and peered upward. She saw corn tassels, the hazy white sky—but no sun to give her direction. She remained unmoving until she heard a noise. A squeak, a chatter, a croak: a squirrel. Rosemary turned right, toward the squirrel.

She plunged from field to forest. The first thing she saw was a luna moth: a pale green moth the size of a saucer. " 'Indeed, it is a strange-disposed time,' " Rosemary told the moth. She rarely saw lunas this late in the season.

She followed the luna moth almost all the way to the river, and then she made her own way along the riverbank. When she saw Con sitting stone-still, absolutely silent, she hesitated for a moment. Then she coughed a little, to announce her presence, and stepped forward.

Con looked around.

Rosemary sat beside her sister. "What is he saying?" she asked.

"That it's a day of shadows without sun. That means there'll be sadness."

Across the river, the Indian stood. He was hardly as tall as A-Two, but his bare arms and legs were corded and strong. While Rosemary stared, he did something that he had never done before: He nodded at Rosemary as if he knew her, as if he had always known her. Then he disappeared.

"I didn't mean to make him go away," Rosemary breathed.

"He isn't far. Did Mama send you?"

"No." And Rosemary brought her attention back to her sister. "No. Mama's talking to Papa about whether or not I should be baptized. That's why I came to talk to you. Do *you* think I should be baptized?"

"Yes."

"Have you been baptized?"

"No, but for me it doesn't matter. I think it will matter for you. You live so much amongst other people, far more so than I."

"I don't know if I want to be baptized," Rosemary confided. "Not if Mrs. Bathsheba is the one behind it all."

"Baptism and Mrs. Bathsheba—they're not one and the same. I've read you the stories; you've read them yourself. One of the reasons John baptized people was to prepare them for goodness."

"I don't think Mrs. Bathsheba wants anything good to happen to anybody."

"She is not what baptism is."

Rosemary frowned, thinking. "Mrs. DiAngeli's baby was baptized."

"And Mrs. DiAngeli is good," said Con. "Mrs. DiAngeli is someone who wants only what is good for her baby."

When Rosemary finally arrived home, her mother was waiting for her. "Rosie," said Althea, "I want you to wash. And to wear your petticoat." Althea frowned at Rosemary's bare legs. "Your shift has become much, much too short."

"It's indecent," said A-Two from her loom.

"And comb your hair," said Althea.

"Then we're going to the mill?"

"You're going, alone. If you need an adult to act for you, your friend Mrs. DiAngeli will do."

"We have work to do," said A-Two. "Our work, and now yours, too."

"That's enough, girls," said Althea.

"I didn't say anything," Rosemary protested.

"Wash your face," Althea directed.

By the time Rosemary left the house, she felt almost pretty. A-Two had combed her hair, braided it, and then looped it into an adult-looking crown. "If you lose one of my hairpins . . . ," A-Two threatened.

"I won't lose *anything*," Rosemary promised. She walked carefully down the wagon path, afraid to turn her head too much or too quickly. Before she reached the squire's turnoff, she took off her petticoat. In this heat, even her shift weighed too much. The little sparrows sitting on the squire's rail fence held their wings out from their bodies. Their beaks gaped open; their eyes looked glazed.

There were almost forty hot children at the millpond: The oldest was Benjie's fifteen-year-old cousin, Sarah; the youngest was a farmer's baby whom Althea had delivered only days before. Rosemary, at the outskirts of the crowd, pulled her petticoat back over her shift. She saw Mrs. Bathsheba, all the women from the mill, and farmers' wives from both up and down the river, but nowhere did she see Mrs. Di-Angeli. She hesitated, not sure what to do, until Benjie appeared at her side.

"They're going to do the babies first," he said. "And then we're supposed to stand in line. Frankie's gone to get the preacher."

"What is he like?" Rosemary asked.

"A knave," said Benjie. "A whoreson. He drank all the coffee this morning—didn't leave any for anybody else. He said it was God's gift to him, to give him energy for saving souls. He's shortsighted, too. He practically had to put his nose on the rim when he poured milk into the cup."

"Really?" Rosemary was interested.

"Look," said Benjie, "here he comes."

The preacher wasn't wearing his hat this day. His hair stuck out all around his head like a dark cloud. Frankie preceded him up the path; Laffer followed. Laffer was carrying a dipping gourd.

"O Lord!" Mrs. Bathsheba cried out.

"O Lord," the preacher responded. He spoke, he didn't shout; but his voice carried as far as the trees. Rosemary was impressed. "Bless us this day. Give us these children that we give unto Thee. Let them grow tall and stalwart as Thy holy soldiers."

"That's us," said Rosemary.

"Madam," the preacher said, lowering his voice just a little. Mrs. Bathsheba walked to the edge of the millpond with her two smallest children, one on each arm. The preacher took the gourd from Laffer and dipped it into the pond. "I baptize thee . . ." He stopped.

Mrs. Bathsheba bowed her head and spoke softly.

"Isaac and Esau," Benjie said into Rosemary's ear.

"Isaac and Esau," the preacher confirmed.

Paulie Proctor was baptized, as were the babies from the farms. Then the older children lined up, beginning with little Ruth Bathsheba.

"I baptize thee Ruth," said the preacher.

"I baptize thee Lafayette," he told Laffer.

"I baptize thee Rosemary." A whole gourdful

of wonderfully cool water poured into her crown and spread over her face and neck.

"Ah," Rosemary sighed, refreshed. She stepped aside.

"Watch," Benjie whispered into her ear. He got back into line, behind Martha. Rosemary was puzzled: Benjie had already been baptized.

Once again Benjie stood before the preacher. "I baptize thee . . . ," the preacher said.

"William," said Benjie.

"William," the preacher finished. He doused Benjie again.

Rosemary quickly looked around. Benjie's mother was talking to the farm wives, her mouth moving at a furious rate. Mrs. Olivia Proctor stood a little apart from the other women, shaking her head as if in disagreement.

"I told you he was shortsighted." This time Benjie's whisper was gleeful. "You try it."

Rosemary found a place between Wash and Elizabeth. "I baptize thee . . . ," said the preacher.

"Mary Rose," said Rosemary, and once again she was refreshed.

"Alexander," said Benjie.

"Maria Constance," said Rosemary.

"King Lear," said Benjie.

They wove in and out of the line, like ribbons in a braid, in competition to get the most names. Benjie was ahead, with eight baptisms, when his mother—at a word from a watching farm wife—left the huddle of women and marched down to the pond to grab his ear. "Come away!" she whispered, and she dragged Benjie back to the adults. Rosemary followed. "You devil, you!"

"No," said one of the laughing farm wives, "he's holier than the others. He'll probably become a preacher."

Benjie looked worried.

"Not this one," Mrs. Bathsheba said, and she shook Benjie's ear furiously. "Never this one. Laffer, maybe. But not this one."

When Rosemary returned home, she was in a cheerful mood. "There's going to be a big meeting," she told her mother, "beside the millpond, after supper. People are bringing cakes and pies, and some of the men are already making torches. The preacher's going to talk."

"Oh, dear," said Althea.

"Who is going to be there?" asked A-Two.

"Everybody. I've already told the Smalls and the squire."

"The Smalls?" said A-Two. "Are they going? All of them?"

"When I left the squire's, he was telling Tillie to make the biggest cake she could. She said she didn't have enough time to make one that big."

"Oh, dear," Althea said again.

"Are we going, Mama? May we go?"

"I think," said Althea, "that we have to."

All the family, except for Con, left the house soon after supper, when the shadows should have been long and narrow. But the sky was still hot and white, and the evening shadows, like the daytime shadows, were faint and formless. "Did you see the sun today?" Colin asked Althea. "Did you see it even once?"

Rosemary walked behind her parents and beside A-Two. A-Two carried her special cake. Rosemary carried A-Two's shoes—the payment A-Two had demanded for loaning out her hairpins. "You look fine," Rosemary judged, for she

189

hadn't seen A-Two dressed so well since the Independence Day ball. "You'd look finer in your new gown."

"It isn't finished yet," A-Two said regretfully. "If it had been, I would have worn it." When they reached the Smalls' turnoff, she took a long look up their track, and then another long look down the road toward the mill.

"Do you want your shoes?" Rosemary asked.

"Not yet."

It wasn't until they had almost reached the mill that A-Two saw Thomas. "Now!" she said, and Rosemary set the shoes on the ground and took the cake from her sister's hands.

"I don't know," said Rosemary. "I don't know if it will work."

"What are you talking about?" A-Two snapped. "Give me that cake." And with her face suddenly soft smiles, with her bosom pushed forward, A-Two pranced over to the little group of which the Small family was the core.

Rosemary sighed.

"Rosie?" Althea looked over her shoulder. "Stay with us."

Rosemary moved up next to her parents. The clearing before the mill and around the millpond was crowded with people from up and down the river. Wagons were pushed back into the trees; ladies served late suppers to families sitting in, and gathered around, the wagon beds. Some of the men carried torches, as yet unlit. Mrs. Bathsheba presided over a long makeshift table on which almost every arriving woman set down a pie or cake.

"I haven't seen it this crowded," said Colin, "since the very first Independence Day celebration."

Mrs. DiAngeli, holding a cake the size of a small mountain, laid her offering on the table.

"Mama!" Rosemary pulled at her mother's arm.

"Stay with us, Rosie," said Althea.

All Rosemary could do was wave, which she did with both arms, standing on her toes. Mrs. DiAngeli waved back.

"I think," said Colin, "that the squire wants us to listen."

The squire stood on the mill steps, waving his arms just as Rosemary had done. He said something that nobody heard. "Louder!" shouted a man from the crowd. And then the doorway behind the squire filled with a shadow as high as the sill. The preacher, his hair still in disarray, stepped through.

"Good people," he said. His voice filled the air like a heavy smoke. He wasn't shouting, he wasn't screaming, he was only talking; but everybody heard. "*God's* people! I have come to this wilderness to bring you the word of the Lord. My text today is One Samuel: 'Put away the wizards out of the land.' I speak of your society. I speak of your souls. I speak of the evil that you harbor within and amongst yourselves. Let us pray."

"Hello," said Benjie to Rosemary. Everybody in the crowd but the very smallest children and their mothers—and Benjie—had a bowed head and folded hands.

" 'Our Father . . . ,' " Rosemary recited. Then, to Benjie: "There's blood on your shirt."

"Pa whipped me. Look." Benjie raised his shirt. "It bled some."

"Ooh," Rosemary said to the welts.

"Mama told him about the baptizing. He said

I can get saved only once tonight. I wonder what it's like, getting saved."

"I don't know," said Rosemary. She hadn't known that saving would be on the evening's program. "What are we being saved from?"

"Wizards and witches," said Benjie. "Listen to him."

"Born in innocence, we are plunged into sin by the devil's minions," the preacher declared. "The devil is amongst us always, in every disguise!"

"What does he mean?" Rosemary wondered.

"Hush," said Althea to both Rosemary and Benjie.

"All ye who have yielded to sin, repent!" the preacher roared. "All ye who have embraced the devil's darkness, give yourselves, now, up unto the Lord!"

"I repent," screamed a woman, "I repent," and she pushed her way forward through the crowd.

"And I!" said a man.

"And I!" shouted Mrs. Bathsheba. "Lord, Lord, give me grace!"

They, and other people, lined up before the

mill steps, under the hand of the reaching preacher. "Repent!" the preacher demanded. "Banish all evil from your lives!" Half the people before him fell on their knees; one woman fainted. "You, madam," the preacher said sternly to the first woman in line, "do you repent your sins? Will you shun all evil? Do you now throw yourself upon the mercy of the Lord?"

"I do," she wailed.

The preacher touched her on the head, and she collapsed. The preacher looked at the next person in line.

"This is much more exciting than baptizing," Rosemary said—to Benjie, she thought. But when she looked around, Benjie wasn't there. Rosemary edged away from her parents. She meant to go to the front of the crowd, where Benjie was no doubt standing in line before the preacher, welts and all. But instead of going forward, she was pushed to the side. Too many people were moving in too many directions all at once. Suddenly a strong arm surrounded Rosemary. "You don't want to be crushed," said Mr. DiAngeli. "We have some madness here."

Rosemary smiled up at him. "I'm looking for Benjie," she said. "He's going to get into trouble soon."

"Do you want to help him?" Mr. DiAngeli inquired. "Or do you want to watch?"

Rosemary considered the alternatives. "I want to watch."

"Then stay with me. Here," and her protector lifted her onto a stump. "Can you see better now? Can you see Maria?"

Rosemary could see wonderfully. Mrs. Di-Angeli, with other mothers and tiny children, stood behind the protection of the refreshment table. The line before the preacher had looped halfway around the millpond; the people in line swayed back and forth as if hooked one to the other. The squire, who apparently still thought himself that evening's host, handed torches to unrepentant boys and men and sent them out to stand in a big circle around the crowd. Benjie, in line, must have changed his mind about what he wanted to do, because he slid away from the other swayers and fought his way to the squire.

The shadows, which before had been so soft

and formless, by now had disappeared into dusk. The dusk deepened into a strange, pale night. Whenever the line shortened to only a few people, the preacher raised his voice again. "Repent, ye sinners!" he cried. "Repent, or be damned to hell!"

The torches burned straight upward, to a sky that held no moon or stars, to a sky that was ash-gray.

"Nothing looks right," Rosemary said.

Mr. DiAngeli didn't answer. He wasn't listening. He didn't seem to be listening to anybody, not even the preacher. He was staring, blindly, straight ahead.

"Mr. DiAngeli?" Rosemary touched his shoulder. And then something dreadful happened, something that she had longed to see but hoped never to see again. Mr. DiAngeli laid his head back, stuck his tongue out, and threw his arms out so fiercely that the people he struck gasped with pain.

"What?" said somebody.

Like a wild man, like a beast, like a rabid dog, Mr. DiAngeli fell to the ground. He rolled and thrashed and struck and kicked. People pushed backward, leaving him and Rosemary in a circle of awe.

"Get Mrs. Weston," a man called.

"Here's the preacher," said someone else.

The preacher stepped through the crowd and into the open circle. He was as tall as a tree and darker than a shadow. He looked down on Mr. DiAngeli from his great height, and he spoke. "Sinner," he said coldly. "Tormented by devils. Touched by a witch. This man beds with evil."

A woman in the crowd gasped. "No," she said slowly. It was Mrs. Olivia Proctor.

Alone on her stump, Rosemary wept. Desperately she looked for her mother. She saw Mrs. DiAngeli, now kneeling within the confines of the circle, sobbing, baby Flavio clutched to her breast. She saw Mrs. Bathsheba, smiling, nodding, pointing her finger at the horrible tableau.

"Mama." Rosemary moved her lips; she couldn't say the sound. And then she saw her mother, stopped in the crowd, staring at the preacher. Even from a distance, Rosemary could tell: Althea's face was taut with horror.

CHAPTER 11

Differences

"He called Mr. DiAngeli a sinner! He said Mr. DiAngeli had been touched by a witch!" It was the following evening; Con was milking the cow. Rosemary had her own chores to do, but instead, for the fifth time, she was telling Con about the preaching. "Mr. DiAngeli is a good man!"

"Yes," Con agreed sadly. "He is a good man."

"Then why did the preacher say those things?"

"Because of what he saw and what he'd heard. Because the DiAngelis are different." After five times, Con's response was still the same.

"No!" Rosemary still refused to believe it.

She stood, brushed the straw from her backside, and left her sister alone.

She fed and bedded the chickens, then wandered into the house. Her mother and A-Two were there, working within the fading light of the open front door. They were finishing A-Two's new gown. A-Two wore her shoes; she stood straight and tall. Althea sat on the floor, sewing the hem. A-Two's face was flushed; she was pleased with herself. Althea was grumbling. "Too much bosom," she was saying. "Really, A-Two, I think you are showing much too much bosom."

"I have extra lace. I'll add a little lace if you insist. But oh, Mama! I have never, ever had such a pretty gown!" If Althea hadn't been holding on to the hem, A-Two would have twirled. "Rosie!" she said gaily. "More lace?" And she pointed toward her bosom.

"You could go to the squire's house," said Rosemary. "You could look in his mirror."

"May I, Mama? May I, tomorrow?"

"I suppose," said Althea. "Yes. But A-Two, we have to do something for Rosie."

They turned their attention to Rosemary. Rosemary stood like a slave for sale, watching their eyes move up and down her body.

"She's grown two inches," said Althea, "maybe three."

"She'll have a bosom soon," A-Two remarked.

Rosemary looked down at her chest.

"There is the linen you wove for your father's shirts," Althea remembered.

"I saved some dandelion dye."

"That will be pretty." Althea nodded in approval. "Would you like that, Rosie?"

"Yes."

But Althea continued to study her youngest daughter as if Rosemary were a calf, a colt, a kid. "You're growing, Rosie," she mused. "You're growing so very fast. Time comes down upon us so quickly. There are things you and I have to talk about. But not right now. For now, I want you to go to the squire's with A-Two tomorrow. I want you to look at yourself, to see the changes."

The next morning, walking along the wagon path, A-Two actually sang. " 'They shall be as happy, happy as they're fair. Love, love shall fill all, all the places of care!' " she trilled.

Rosemary, by choice, walked six steps behind.

"Hello, Thomas!" A-Two called out.

Thomas Small, working in one of the squire's fields, raised his hand in a curt gesture and continued with his work.

"He still doesn't like you very much," Rosemary volunteered.

"You know *nothing*," A-Two retorted. But silent now, she turned up the squire's track.

The squire was behind his house, back in the peach orchard, examining the fruit. "Another two weeks and they'll be ripe," he said, sounding well satisfied.

A-Two civilly but impatiently agreed.

"The mirror?" said the squire. "Of course! And A-Two, there's a letter for you, from Caroline. Just came yesterday. I've been meaning to send Seth over with it. Now, where did I put it? Ask Tillie if she knows."

"Yes, Squire," said A-Two. "Thank you."

While A-Two changed her clothes in Caroline's room, Rosemary stood before the mirror alone. She stared at herself, wondering what she was supposed to see. She stepped forward, close enough to discover that there were tiny hairs on the tip of her nose. She stepped backward, so that she had a view of her whole self from head to ankle. Her shift was indeed very short. Rosemary stood, looking at a girl who resembled every other girl-child along the river. And then she was bustled over to a narrow edge of the mirror by the newly arrived A-Two.

"The letter was on Caroline's bed. The squire would never have remembered it there. Oh! Look at me!"

Rosemary looked, politely. A-Two tied her sash a little tighter; she smoothed the delicate cloth over her thighs. The sight was new to A-Two, but Rosemary had seen it often these past weeks.

Bored, Rosemary began to play with the mirror. She pretended she had never seen A-Two before. She pretended she had never seen herself. Her eyes, a stranger's eyes, peered at new reflections. And then, suddenly, Rosemary saw what Althea had wanted her to see. She saw a girl-child who was no longer a child. Through the loose weave of Rosemary's shift, the shadow of her body curved: in at the waist, out at the hips. Rosemary turned sideways: There was a tiny rising on her chest. She was no longer what she had been; she was something new. She frowned.

"Read the letter," A-Two ordered. "Read it out loud."

Rosemary obediently opened the letter. " 'August the third, 1790.' "

"Go on!"

" 'Dear A-Two, I cannot tell you how happy I am! My dear Roger loves me! He is even now writing to Papa to ask permission for our marriage. With Papa's consent, we will be married here, in New Bern. Oh, A-Two, I cannot tell you how much I will miss you! My new life will be out here by the sea, with Roger. His friends will be my friends. But you, my dearest, most cherished A-Two, will never leave my heart,' " Rosemary finished.

A-Two had stopped moving. Her hands, at her sash, were suddenly limp. Her shoulders had fallen forward. She still stared at herself, but not with eagerness and pleasure. Her face, her expression, had become shaped by new emotions: some grief, much humility. "Caroline is getting married," she said softly. *"Before me."*

"Well!" the squire boomed. "What a pretty girl!"

A-Two's body straightened; her face didn't change.

"Lovely," said the squire. "Just lovely." He stood at the room's entrance, beaming at them both. "Unusual, though. What do you call it?"

"It's just a gown," A-Two said dispiritedly.

"It's going to catch *everybody's* eye," the squire said heartily. "Are you girls going straight home?"

"I am," said A-Two, "in a minute. As soon as I change out of my gown."

"Mama didn't say I had to hurry," Rosemary told the squire.

"Then maybe you'll do me a favor. Have you read my Caroline's special news?"

"Yes," A-Two sighed.

"I knew she would want you to hear it from her. She's found herself a husband! What do you think of that? A good man, her mother tells me, able to provide. I can't say that I agree with his politics . . . but they're waiting for my answer. I'll seal the letter right now, and Rosie will take it to the mill."

"All right," said Rosemary.

"We'll have a party," the squire promised. "A big party. A-Two, you wear that gown!"

Rosemary could have gone straight to the mill; instead, she turned left at the millpond and ran up the hill to the schoolhouse. "Mrs. DiAngeli!" she called. "Mrs. DiAngeli!" The door was open, so she stepped right in. Mrs. DiAngeli was crooning over the cradle beside the big bed. Rosemary put her hand to her mouth. "I'm sorry," she whispered.

"It's all right," Mrs. DiAngeli whispered back. "His eyes are closed. He's asleep."

"Caroline Chalmers is getting married." Rosemary continued to whisper.

"To whom?"

"Her beau in New Bern."

"Really?" Mrs. DiAngeli stepped away from the cradle. She began to walk toward Rosemary, but then thought of something, turned, and reached for an object on the shelf beside the bed. "Let's go outside."

Out in the sunlight, Rosemary looked first at her friend's hands—whatever she carried was wrapped in an old apron—and then at Mrs. DiAngeli's face. "You look horrible!" Rosemary blurted out. "Are you ill? Should I ask Mama to visit you?"

"No." Mrs. DiAngeli sat down on one of the leftover school benches. "Don't ask her. She might not want to come."

"Of course she will come." Instead of sitting, Rosemary stood in front of Mrs. DiAngeli. She tried to be her mother, looking into an ill person's face. She saw pallor, strain, and a tiny flicking of the eyelid. "I know Mama will come."

"Benjie was here this morning," Mrs. DiAngeli remarked, as though they had been talking about something else.

"Did he make you sick?" Rosemary wondered.

"No, of course not. But he gave me these." Mrs. DiAngeli reached into her pocket and held out her cupped hand: Benjie's wooden fish, the two apple-worm bobbers, a carved lady doll.

"Those are their toys!" Rosemary exclaimed. "The ones you made for the Bathsheba children!"

"Benjie gave them back. All of them."

"Why?"

Mrs. DiAngeli's shoulders slumped. She didn't answer the question. Instead she said, "I made something for you—just finished it. But perhaps you won't want it, either."

"Of *course* I will want it!"

Mrs. DiAngeli unwound the apron from the object on her lap. Rosemary held her breath. It was a box—a perfect, splendid, absolutely wonderful box; a box that was meant for treasures, because it was a treasure itself. "Ohhh!" Rosemary let her breath go. It was the most beautiful box she had ever seen, more beautiful, even, than Mrs. DiAngeli's lamp box. Rosemary tried to look up into Mrs. DiAngeli's eyes, to say thank you, but instead her hands reached for the box.

She touched, she saw: the carved roses, the carved dragonflies. The roses twined about the box as though they grew from a stem just below.

The dragonflies darted in and out of the vine: some resting on a leaf or thorn, others flying, two battling in midair.

"It's so real!" Rosemary breathed.

"What?" asked Mrs. DiAngeli.

"It's beautiful," Rosemary said more loudly, and this time she did meet her friend's eyes. "It's the most beautiful, *beautiful* thing I have ever seen!"

"It's made of walnut," said Mrs. DiAngeli. "It will last forever." She was almost smiling.

"I will keep it forever," Rosemary declared.

Mrs. DiAngeli's smile faded. "Will your mama let you keep it?" she asked.

"Of course she will. She'll think it's beautiful, too. Why wouldn't she let me keep it?"

Mrs. DiAngeli closed her eyes. A tear rolled down her cheek in a little groove that Rosemary now saw had been formed by earlier tears. "You're crying! Why?"

"Because," said Mrs. DiAngeli. "Because." And she wouldn't explain further. Instead, she wrapped the box up in the apron and sent Rosemary home.

Rosemary would have obeyed, but she still had the squire's letter to deliver. She climbed the steps to the mill with her bundle under her arm, wondering if, once inside, she might unwrap her box and show it off. But she was quite sure—for a reason she did not fully understand—that that would be exactly the wrong thing to do.

The miller, when he saw her, was his usual teasing self. "Good morning, miss," he greeted. "What is your prediction of the ginseng crop this year?"

"Caroline Chalmers is getting married." Rosemary handed over the letter. "This is the squire's permission."

"Well!" The miller was pleased. "That is good news. Will they be married here or in New Bern?"

"New Bern, I think. But the squire will have a party here."

"Another party," said an old man sitting in the grain sack parlor. "My, but this has been a summer for festivities. Now, when I was young—"

"You were never young, Mr. Brady," said someone else. "You've always been as old as Methuselah."

"Now, when I was young—," the elderly man persisted, but at that moment Mr. DiAngeli walked into the mill. Everybody fell silent. Only Rosemary smiled.

"Hello," she said, made shy by all that silence.

"Rosie." Mr. DiAngeli ruffled her hair. "Have any merchants come by today?" he asked the miller.

"No," the miller replied.

"If one does come by, please place an order for me. I want twenty pounds of sixpenny nails." Mr. DiAngeli nodded at the men in the parlor and then left the mill.

"He wants to *buy* his nails," said old Mr. Brady. "The ones our smith makes aren't good enough."

"My wife says that his brat was spawned by the devil," said another man.

Rosemary stared.

"How many children were baptized that day?" someone asked.

"Fifty, fifty-five—that's what the preacher said. And not one of them named DiAngeli."

"Evil." One of the farmers shook his head. "Even his barrels are touched by evil."

"I had a sense the first time I saw them," said someone else. "I had a sense there would be trouble."

Rosemary turned and ran. "Rosie," the miller called after her. "A chip?" But she didn't stop. She ran outside and stood sputtering, angry, ready to do war with the world. And then she saw Benjie.

"You!" she spat. She advanced upon him as if he were the meanest, ugliest creature that she had ever seen. "You! You made her cry."

"What?" said Benjie. And then, "I didn't mean to."

"You didn't mean to," Rosemary mimicked contemptuously.

"I had to do it, Rosie. Mama made me."

"Why? Why did you have to do it? Why did she make you?"

"She said that our toys were the devil's playthings, carved by a witch." Benjie sighed.

"A witch!"

"The toys were too perfect, Mama said. And they *were* perfect, you know that, Rosie. Mama said that, being so perfect, they couldn't have been made by human hands."

"That's a lie!"

"Mama said they weren't true gifts, meant to please," Benjie continued miserably. "She said they were the devil's devices, meant to steal our souls."

"And you believed her? You believed that?" Rosemary was incredulous.

"I had to take them back, Rosie." Benjie tried hard to explain. "I still haven't healed from my last whipping. I'm not ready for another one, not yet."

"You coward." Rosemary seethed. She stepped backward, away from someone who had once almost been a friend. "You knave. You whoreson!"

"Rosie!"

But Rosemary had spun around and fled. She ran furiously, leaving a wind behind her. "The two daughters in *King Lear* . . . ," she panted out loud. "Now, *they* were evil. And the serpent in the garden. And the Gorgons, of course." As

Rosemary's list grew longer and longer, she saw less and less resemblance between true evil and the DiAngelis. Her anger grew until her body and soul were fire red. By the time she saw her mother, working in the herb garden, Rosemary was ready to explode.

"Mama!" she shouted sharply. "Mama!"

Althea looked up.

"Mama, they are horrible! They are all horrible!"

"Who?" Althea asked mildly.

"Everybody. Mrs. Bathsheba. The men at the mill."

"Oh." Althea had been cutting savory and thyme to hang over the fireplace and let dry for the winter, but now she stopped.

"They're saying things, terrible things. That Mr. DiAngeli is evil! That Mrs. DiAngeli is a witch!"

"Oh, no!"

Rosemary dropped to her haunches beside the pile of cut herbs. "I hate them," she said fiercely. "They're stupid."

"Yes," Althea agreed.

Rosemary was surprised. She hadn't expected

her mother to agree with her, not so readily, not when she was insulting adults.

"It is stupidity," said Althea. "But it's also fear. They're afraid."

"Of what? Nobody's sweeter than Mrs. Di-Angeli. Nobody's kinder than Mr. DiAngeli."

"They are afraid," said Althea, "of what they don't understand."

"But they know Mrs. DiAngeli!" Rosemary protested. "They know Mrs. DiAngeli almost as well as they know us!"

"Yes," Althea agreed.

Rosemary stopped yelling. Her mother knelt in the herb garden, her knife in her lap, her eyes both tired and kind.

"Mrs. DiAngeli is different," Rosemary said slowly.

"Yes."

"She can do things with her hands. Things that nobody else can do, even if they try."

"Yes."

"Just as you can do things. You and Con." Rosemary looked at her mother.

Althea nodded.

It was as if there were a tremor, a movement,

a slight shifting deep within the core of the earth. "Danger," Rosemary whispered. "Papa said it was dangerous."

"Not for other people," Althea immediately corrected. "Only for us."

"For us," said Rosemary. And in that moment her world changed.

CHAPTER 12

Witches

"It is a beautiful box," said Althea. "A beautiful piece of work. Art, I think."

"I am glad you like it," said Mrs. DiAngeli.

"Rosie will treasure it forever. And her daughters after her."

Mrs. DiAngeli smiled, looking relieved. She touched the pitcher of cool sumac tea on the table and said, "May I pour more for you?"

"Thank you," said Althea.

"Thank you," said Rosemary. At the end of Mrs. DiAngeli's table, on Rosemary's side, sat a large blueberry pie. Rosemary and her mother had made the pie early that morning. As soon as the pie was cool enough to carry, they had brought it through the warm, moist morning air, all the way down the wagon path and up the little hill to the schoolhouse.

"Rosemary tells me," said Althea, "that one of your great-grandmothers was an artist in Italy."

"Yes," Mrs. DiAngeli replied. "I never knew her, of course. That was many, many years before I was born."

"My six-times-great-grandmother was a famous weaver," Althea said. "A Scotswoman. She came to this continent during Oliver Cromwell's time and settled in Rhode Island. A most unusual person. My daughter Constance is named after her."

"It was my parents' parents who came to America," said Mrs. DiAngeli. "We haven't been here so very long."

"Long enough to be good citizens," Althea said staunchly, "which I know you to be."

"Thank you." But Mrs. DiAngeli sighed. "My husband, Flavio, is out working on the land that he hopes to make into a farm. He found spicebush yesterday—"

"Spicebush means good soil," Rosemary interjected.

217

"Yes," Mrs. DiAngeli agreed. She clasped her hands on top of the table; she held them together so tightly that her knuckles turned white. "Please tell me, Mrs. Weston—if you don't mind speaking frankly—do you think we have a future here?"

Althea didn't respond immediately. Rosemary was anxious. "I hope . . . I think . . . that people will soon forget all the disturbances of these last several days," Althea finally said. "Surely something else will occur to interest them—even if it is only their own tasks and duties. With the preacher gone, with all the excitement that he brought gone, surely people will return to their senses."

"That's what Flavio says. He says the district needs a cooper; they can't be so foolish as to forget their own needs."

"Exactly," Althea agreed.

Mrs. DiAngeli managed a smile. "So you think it will be all right?"

"Oh, I hope so." Althea was fervent. "For your sake, and ours, I do hope so."

"You have been so kind."

"No." Althea corrected her neighbor. "No, it

218

is you who have been kind. You have made this summer special for Rosie. You have helped her to grow. I am grateful."

Rosemary looked at her mother with surprise.

Mrs. DiAngeli actually grinned. "We have had our good times, haven't we?" she said to Rosemary. "Must you really leave?" she added, for Althea was standing up.

"Yes. We have work waiting at home. But we'll come again. I hope you'll enjoy the pie."

"Oh, we will!" When Mrs. DiAngeli waved goodbye from her doorway, she was almost cheerful.

"I'll come see you tomorrow," Rosemary called over her shoulder. To Althea, she said, "That was good, Mama. That was a *good* visit."

"Yes," said Althea. "Yes. But oh, Rosie!" She stood irresolute for a moment at the bottom of the hill. She looked in the direction of the smith's house; she contemplated the miller's house. She chose to visit the miller's.

On this day the miller's family was inside. "Baking," said the miller's wife, "before the day gets too hot."

"But it's hot already," sighed Mrs. Olivia

Proctor. "We had a late start. Paulie fell into the fire. Will you look at him, Mrs. Weston?"

Althea examined the red blister on Paulie's arm.

"We pulled him out directly," said Miss Nancy Proctor.

"It's not a bad burn," Althea assured mother, aunt, and grandmother. "Have you treated it?"

"With a poultice," said Mrs. Olivia Proctor. "Rum, onions, and cornmeal."

"Yes," Althea approved. "That was the right thing to do. Now you'll want to keep it clean, very clean."

"I'm so glad you came by," said Mrs. Olivia Proctor. "I was so worried."

"She burnt the bread," said the miller's wife.

"Only two loaves."

"Rosemary and I have been visiting Mrs. Di-Angeli," said Althea.

Mrs. Olivia Proctor looked worried. "I don't know if you should have done that."

"Of course I should have done it," Althea responded. "She's a lovely young woman, very kind."

"She is nice," Mrs. Olivia Proctor said doubt-
fully. "And I did like her so much."

"You should still like her," Althea said
stoutly.

"But the preacher . . . you heard what he
said!"

"He said nothing against Maria DiAngeli,"
Althea reminded them all.

"But he said that Mr. DiAngeli bedded with
evil!"

"Stuff and nonsense," Miss Nancy Proctor
snorted.

"Don't be rude, Nancy," the miller's wife instructed her daughter. She turned to Althea.
"There may be some truth to what the preacher
said, Mrs. Weston. Why, only a few days before
the DiAngelis arrived here, old Daniel Brady
saw a bolt of lightning bend back against itself
in the sky. That wasn't natural. It could only
have been done by the devil's hands."

Rosemary swallowed a gasp; she turned to her
mother.

"Pish," said Miss Nancy Proctor. "Piddle.
Old Daniel Brady has been seeing things since

his seventy-fifth birthday, fifteen years ago. You know that, Mama."

"And about the same time," the miller's wife continued, "a two-headed calf was almost born at the Smalls'. Your husband was there, Mrs. Weston; he saw it. More devil's work. An omen, I'm sure."

"My husband saw the unfortunate and difficult death of a cow and her calf. Neither that nor old Mr. Brady's fantasies had *anything* to do with the DiAngelis!" Althea was emphatic. She and Rosemary said their goodbyes and left.

For once Rosemary was silent as they walked up the wagon path. Silent, until she was absolutely certain that nobody was within a mile of listening. Then: "It was you who turned back the lightning, Mama, the night the Smalls' cow died. So that our farm wouldn't burn."

"Oh, Rosie." And Rosemary saw upon her mother's face some of the horror that had been there the night of the preaching. "I have to tell myself and tell myself: Everything has its consequences!" Althea struggled to compose her voice, her face. "Go into the forest," she directed. "I want to make an ointment for Paulie Proctor's burn. I'll need some witch hazel."

Witch hazel: the one plant that flowered at Christmas; the plant that, in the summer, was dark with sharp galls like black, pointed hats; the plant that, unlike the other plants of the forest, chose the poorest of soils. Rosemary found a spindly bush growing out of a rock.

"You help people to heal," she told the bush, "and yet they call you 'witch.' "

She returned home carrying her twigs, her stems. Stepping out from the trees, the first thing she saw was a long piece of pink cloth— the cloth for her new shift—laid out on the wheat stubs to dry. Rosemary followed the cloth almost to the house.

"Rosie," said Althea. Her face, her voice, were normal now. "I need you to help me with the butter."

It was an ordinary afternoon, and an ordinary evening, too. Con came home with the cow. A-Two brought the pink cloth inside. Colin told his family that the Creek Indians, way down in Georgia, had signed an important treaty with President Washington. Everybody ate and talked as if life weren't always changing. And then they went to bed.

Rosemary lay on her pallet with her eyes open to the ceiling. She listened to Con's breathing, to A-Two's murmuring in her sleep. Everything was as it should be. Except for something important: Rosemary no longer felt safe. She put her hands on her breasts, on her waist, on her hips. Then she sat up and took her rose-and-dragonfly treasure box from the chink in the wall. She curled on her side, holding the box like a doll. And fell asleep.

She was awakened by a certainty that something was missing. She lay still for a minute, trying to figure out what was wrong. She heard her father's snoring, A-Two's mumbling. She didn't hear Con. She sat up and looked in the direction of Con's pallet. She put her box aside and crawled to where Con should be. She knew Con wasn't there, but still she patted her hands up and down the length of the bed. She paused for a moment, considering, and then she quietly climbed down the ladder-stairs and tiptoed out of the house.

The back yard was lit by a waning moon that threw the narrowest of shadows. Rosemary stood where her chickens always ate their evening corn. Slowly, she turned in a circle. When she faced the barn, she frowned and stopped. She thought she heard something that wasn't the cow moving in its straw, that wasn't a mouse searching out grain. She followed a streak of moonlight all the way to the barn door.

She really shouldn't have heard anything at all, because the cow stood on almost bare ground, ruminating comfortably, and Con, sitting on a pile of straw, was motionless. "Hello," Rosemary whispered.

"Rosie," said Con.

Rosemary took that as an invitation to sit on the straw beside her sister. "Are you talking to the cow?" she asked.

"Yes," said Con. "Well, no. Cows don't have words."

"Then how do you talk?"

"We share."

"How?"

"It's like touching." Con put her arm around

her little sister. "We feel each other's minds—I guess. Feel what the other feels, think what the other thinks."

Rosemary tried to think as a cow would think. She couldn't. "No one," she said, "can do what you do."

"I know." Con sighed.

"But what you do isn't evil," Rosemary assured her sister. "Never. Not at all."

"Not at all," Con agreed, and her arm tightened around Rosemary's shoulders.

The next morning, when Rosemary awoke again, she found herself in her bed. She didn't remember returning there. The bedroom loft was almost bright with light: Althea had let her sleep late. Downstairs, only A-Two was still in the house, leaning over the table that had been cleared of everything but Rosemary's pink cloth. "Stand here," A-Two said as soon as she saw her sister. She measured the distance between Rosemary's shoulders. "Put out your arm."

Rosemary stood, sleep still in her eyes, while A-Two measured her body up, down, and around. When A-Two was finished, Rosemary broke a hunk of still-warm corn bread from the skillet near the banked fire. She sat down on a stool. "Is Mama gone?" she asked.

"In the garden."

"Papa?"

"In the fields. Con's with him."

"Con couldn't sleep last night."

"Con is who she is. She can't change." A-Two began to cut the cloth.

"What do you mean?"

"I mean," said A-Two, "that you should help me. Hold down this corner."

Rosemary obeyed.

A-Two relented. "Have you ever wondered why Con hardly ever leaves our farm? Why she never goes to balls and parties? She's afraid. She's afraid other people will learn too much about her."

"Mama goes."

"They're not the same, Mama and Con."

Rosemary nodded. Not the same, but both different from everybody else. "Con said that someday I might be able to do what she does."

"You'll know when you're a woman." A-Two finished cutting out a long pink piece. "That's

227

when it's determined: whether you're like Mama and Con, or like Papa and me. I'm glad I'm like me. Stand still and hold this up in front of you."

Rosemary held the piece to her throat. "When will I be a woman?"

"Soon. Very soon, at the rate you're growing." A-Two knelt at Rosemary's feet and began to roll up fabric from the floor. "We'll give you a deep hem," she decided. "You'll have to start wearing a petticoat soon, all the time. Mama has one that I can cut down for you."

"Very pretty," Althea complimented. "Very pretty, indeed." She stood in the doorway with Thomas Small behind her. Thomas held a large, round pound cake that probably weighed ten pounds. "Look who's here."

"Oh!" A-Two wheezed. Rosemary looked down at her sister. A-Two had shrunk closer to the floor, like a sunken bellows.

"It's a beautiful cake," Althea said to Thomas. "I had thought to have you put it on the table. . . ."

"I'll set it on the dresser, ma'am," said Thomas.

"Such an extravagant present!" said Althea.

"Mama wants to thank you for all of your kindness this summer—the milk, the butter, the cheese."

"We were happy to help. How is the new cow?"

"A fine little creature."

"I'm glad. Won't you stay for a slice?"

"Thank you, ma'am, no. I have chores." Thomas walked toward the door; he turned his head back, as if remembering something. "It's a good cake," he said, "but not as tasty as A-Two's."

A-Two, hidden by Rosemary, turned pinker than the fabric that surrounded her. Thomas caught Rosemary's eye. He winked.

"Did you hear that, Mama?" A-Two breathed when Thomas was gone. "Did you hear that?"

"Of course I heard it," Althea replied. "I was standing right here."

"He likes me," A-Two whispered, "maybe."

"I think he has always liked you," said Rosemary. "It's just that you're so difficult."

"Oh, hush," A-Two snapped. "What do you know?"

"Girls," cautioned Althea, but she was smiling. "Perhaps, A-Two, you would like to return Mrs. Small's platter. I can spare you for an hour or two this afternoon."

That afternoon A-Two wore her best bodice and her second-best petticoat. Rosemary, walking down the wagon path beside her sister, wouldn't have minded another conversation; but A-Two was humming a marching song, a tune of both joy and determination. They parted at the Smalls' turnoff. Rosemary continued down the path by herself.

When she saw Benjie at the millpond, she turned her face in the opposite direction. She walked up the mill steps with her nose pointing to the side.

"Ah, Rosie," Benjie said pleadingly from the distance.

Inside the mill, seven men had gathered in the grain sack parlor. The miller, behind his counter, told Rosemary that the expected shipment of coffee hadn't yet arrived. "Thank you," she said primly.

That errand finished, she thought of—but

couldn't figure out any way of—avoiding Benjie outside. She turned her nose to her other shoulder and left the building.

Benjie was at the bottom of the steps, waiting for her. "Rosie," he said, "don't be so angry."

"I hate you," Rosemary said succinctly, and she passed him by.

"I'm sorry I did what I did."

Rosemary strode onward.

"It was wrong," Benjie confessed.

Rosemary slowed down.

"In a way," said Benjie, "you were right. I was a coward."

Rosemary turned to look at him.

"But you don't know my mama when she has her mind made up. And you don't know my pa when he's angry."

"I know them," Rosemary said. "I know them well."

"If I was fifteen or sixteen, I'd run away," said Benjie. "You can't run away when you're twelve."

Rosemary tried to imagine running away herself. "No," she said.

"So can we be friends?"

"Maybe," said Rosemary. "I'm going to visit Mrs. DiAngeli now." It was a test.

"I'll go with you," said Benjie. "My mama doesn't have to know."

"I won't tell her," said Rosemary. "I won't *ever* tell her."

Mrs. DiAngeli was sitting in the sun with her child. "Listen, Baby!" she said. "That bird is a woodpecker." When Mrs. DiAngeli saw Benjie, she stopped smiling. "Why, Benjie," she said.

"Good afternoon, ma'am." Benjie looked very embarrassed.

"Have you come for something?" asked Mrs. DiAngeli.

"A visit," said Benjie. "That other . . . that was my mother."

"Yes," Mrs. DiAngeli sighed. "I know." Neither she nor Benjie looked at the other for a moment. Then Mrs. DiAngeli said, "I made a cobbler this morning. Would you like some?"

"I never say no to food, ma'am," Benjie promptly replied. "Never."

Mrs. DiAngeli smiled. Then she laughed.

"Spoken like a growing boy," she said. "Come inside."

There was also sumac tea inside, and some ham that Benjie thought would be a nice treat before supper. They all ate, and then Rosemary and Mrs. DiAngeli watched Benjie continue. "I could eat all day," he confessed. "Some days I do."

"Flavio ate from the time he was twelve until he turned twenty," said Mrs. DiAngeli. "Then he got married."

Benjie paused in his eating. "That's not what I'm aiming toward."

Mrs. DiAngeli laughed.

It was lovely, Rosemary thought, to hear her friend laugh again. Baby Flavio, on his mother's lap, smiled too. When the air outside darkened, when it was shaken by thunder, Rosemary at first felt cozy and pleased: How nice to be at a table with friends, everybody laughing and eating, all of them sheltered from the fierce-winded world.

"No rain yet," said Benjie.

"Flavio's working on our land." Mrs. DiAngeli was anxious. "I hope he'll hurry home."

233

"My papa's in the fields, too," said Rosemary. "But Con's with him."

"Listen to that wind," said Benjie.

There was a crack of thunder. Baby Flavio cried. "Hush, hush," soothed Mrs. DiAngeli. The thunder was followed by a flash of lightning so bright that for an instant the inside of the schoolhouse turned silver.

"That was close," said Benjie.

Another crack of thunder, another flash of lightning: Rosemary heard and saw them both at the same time.

"Fire!" Mrs. DiAngeli exclaimed. "I smell fire!"

"It's not the house. I don't think it's the house," said Benjie.

Mrs. DiAngeli grabbed her baby. They all ran outside. Behind the schoolhouse an old pine tree rose like a fiery torch into the sky. "It will fall!" said Mrs. DiAngeli.

"No," Rosemary insisted.

But the tip of the pine did fall, right onto the end of the schoolhouse roof, right next to the chimney.

"I'll get help!" Benjie was already running.

"Buckets!" shouted Rosemary. "Where are your buckets?"

Quickly, Mrs. DiAngeli tied baby Flavio into her apron so that he hung from her waist in a sling. Rosemary dipped buckets again and again into the well. Mrs. DiAngeli tossed water as high as she could. Baby Flavio screamed as the cold water fell back on him.

Rosemary lowered a bucket, then pulled; lowered a bucket, then pulled. Miss Nancy Proctor came charging up the hill like a Fury. She pushed a bench to the side of the house and climbed up on it. "Give me that water!" she ordered.

"You'll catch fire yourself up there!" said Mrs. DiAngeli.

"Give me a bucket!"

Miss Nancy Proctor poured water not on the flames but on the still-untouched slopes of the roof.

"I understand!" said Mrs. DiAngeli.

The fire was still blazing, but no longer spreading, when Benjie returned up the hill. From the sound of his voice, from the glance she had of his face, Rosemary could tell that he was weeping. "They won't come!" he said furiously. "They won't come! Here, Rosie, let me do that."

They were a chain now: Benjie, at the well, pulled up bucket after bucket; Rosemary ran the buckets to Mrs. DiAngeli; Mrs. DiAngeli passed the buckets to Miss Nancy Proctor; Miss Nancy Proctor threw water onto the roof. Baby Flavio, bumping on his mother's hip, cried.

They worked as the end of the roof and the back of the house burned. They worked as the pine tree shot out embers and dropped burning sections of limbs and trunk onto the surrounding hillside. They worked as Mr. DiAngeli came running home with Mr. Algernon Proctor behind him. They worked until the rain began to fall. And then, in the deluge, they stopped.

"It's all right, Maria," said Mr. DiAngeli. "We have it now."

What was left of the pine tree smoked like a doused torch. The hillside fires were smoldering, weak. "There's half the house left," said Mr. Algernon Proctor. "Maybe more than half."

Baby Flavio no longer cried; within the confines of the apron he hiccuped and shivered. Mrs. DiAngeli stared at what had been her home, her eyes wide.

"You need a cup of tea, Maria," Miss Nancy Proctor said gently, somehow able to offer comfort even though her face was black, her hair singed, her sleeves and bodice burnt. "Come home with me. Your husband and my brother— they'll see to things."

"No," said Mrs. DiAngeli. She still stared.

"Then at least come out of the rain. I think your house is safe now. Bring your baby out of the rain."

At the mention of her baby, Mrs. DiAngeli looked down. Her whole body softened. She unfastened baby Flavio and hugged him. "Yes," she said, "yes." She looked up, to try to smile, and saw Rosemary. Her voice became kind, even loving. "Go home, Rosie," she said. "Go home."

Rosemary obeyed. She walked down the track alone, her shift indecently wet, her hair sticking to her neck. She concentrated on putting one foot ahead of the other. When she reached the bottom of the hill, she stopped.

Before Rosemary, with her arms stretched out, as if holding back an army, stood Mrs. Bathsheba. The woman's hair and clothing, in this rain, were as wet as Rosemary's. Her face was washed into creases. Her nose, her chin, jutted forward with self-righteous power. Behind her, blocked by her arms, stood the men from the mill, the miller, the miller's wife, and Mrs. Olivia Proctor.

"Shame!" Mrs. Bathsheba hissed. "Shame on you, girl! It is God's will. It is God's word: 'Thou shalt not suffer a witch to live.'"

CHAPTER 13

Rosemary

The buckeyes were always the first harbingers of autumn; their leaves turned brown while the rest of the forest still clung to summer. But now, by mid-September, the leaves of viburnum, maple, dogwood, and countless other plants had grown dry around their edges, were growing pale along their veins.

Rosemary, wearing her new pink shift, sat alone in the forest, beneath the beech trees. Her knees were pulled up to her chest; her shift was pulled down to her feet. She should have been wearing a petticoat—two weeks ago she had found blood between her thighs, and her mother had said that now she must always wear a petticoat. But this was the forest. Nobody could see her. Rosemary was alone with her thoughts and her memories.

" 'Thou shalt not suffer a witch to live.' Exodus, chapter twenty-two, verse eighteen." Con had known exactly where to find those words. "Here, in the Bible." It was the night of the lightning fire, and very late. All the Westons had gathered around the supper table. A-Two, tears in her eyes, had baked another of her special cakes that evening. It sat in the center of the table, untouched.

"The next time," Con told her family, "they will be talking about me."

"Yes," Colin sadly agreed.

"Yes," Althea echoed.

"So I must go."

"No!" Rosemary protested.

"The next time it will be worse," Con explained. "They could do me harm; they might do *you* harm, too, Rosie. Don't regret me too much. It's not all for the bad. I'm going to go search for other people like me. I'm going to find a place where I don't have to hide."

And the next day—the same day that the DiAngelis loaded their wagon with what remained of their belongings and moved away forever—Con had left, too.

"Can't you tell where she is?" Rosemary, in her new loneliness, sometimes asked her mother.

"No." Nowadays, even through her own great sadness, Althea was always watching Rosemary. "You know that I can't see that way. But I do know that Con is safe."

They all knew that Con was safe—that Con was even well—because sometimes, still, a book would begin to move on the little table. The book would lay itself down, would open, the pages would turn. Whenever that happened, Rosemary stopped in her work to stand and read what Con was reading: the words of Jesus, a play, a story about a Greek god. Even Colin watched the pages turn—with unhappiness, not anger or fear.

Deep within the forest, Rosemary sighed and stood. She put her hand to the back of her shift and felt the dampness of last night's rain. A nighttime rain in September meant morning mushrooms. Rosemary was supposed to be gathering mushrooms.

She let her feet pull the rest of her body slowly down the hill. She saw green mushrooms the color of mold on a wooden fence; she walked past them. She bypassed mushrooms as blue as robins' eggs. She saw a white mushroom large enough to sit on, but she didn't stop. She stepped over egg mushrooms that, later on, would break open to release parasols the colors of autumn sunsets. She ignored the little red-capped mushrooms; the white fungus growing like claws from the ground; a slimy orange mound that looked like brain. None of these would do for the evening meal. Thomas Small was coming for supper.

Thomas now ate with the Westons so often that Rosemary saw no reason to treat him as somebody special. But tonight was the squire's promised party. Thomas was escorting A-Two.

A-Two had long since sewn extra lace across the bosom of her new gown. "I don't need to show myself off to *everybody*," she told Rosemary. "Besides, I may want to wear this gown later for something special. Something *very* special." She wouldn't say what or when that special time was to be; instead, she smiled shyly. In all the long years that Rosemary had known A-Two, she had never before known her sister to be shy.

Now, in the forest, Rosemary's feet finally stopped. She bent. From between two tree roots she plucked a little soot-rimmed brown funnel, the color of bark. She put the funnel to her nose and inhaled: The scent was like ripe autumn fruit, like the squire's best wine. This was the mushroom her mother wanted. Rosemary stepped from tree to tree, examining the ground between roots. She gathered as many mushrooms as Althea needed for her family and Thomas; she gathered more, to dry and save.

She reached the river. For several long minutes Rosemary gazed at the opposite shore. She imagined, she almost saw, Con wading across the river; the Indian meeting Con, greeting her; Con disappearing like love and magic into the colors of autumn.

"Goodbye," Rosemary whispered.

"Ro-sie!" A call from the distance: A-Two, impatient for the mushrooms.

"Ro-sie!" Another voice, a teasing voice,

joined A-Two's: Benjie. Benjie often worked at the Weston farm these days, to repay Althea for the mountains of food she gave him. He sometimes slept in the Smalls' shed or the squire's barn. Since the day of the lightning fire, he had not returned to his parents' house.

Rosemary turned toward home. Her back was dry now, and warming. The sunlight that fell into the patchy clearings was almost golden. Rosemary left the forest's edge for her father's meadow; she nearly stepped on a fallen chrysalis. She danced to the side, juggling her basket of mushrooms. Her balance regained, she squatted to look.

It was a stout chrysalis, green and ribbed. Through the thin shell Rosemary could see the pattern of orange-and-black wings. This was a monarch butterfly, meant to overwinter in the forest and emerge full-grown in springtime. But it would die on the ground: stomped upon by a person or cow, eaten by a goat, rotted by rain.

"You should fly south," Rosemary said to the butterfly-to-be. "You should fly with your family and your friends."

She rose, holding the chrysalis, and looked about. Her father and Benjie were fields away. Her mother, kneeling in the garden, was only a blue patterned back.

Rosemary was all alone, and suddenly she was afraid.

Because the moment had come—somehow, she knew: She had a choice. She could try and fail, and then she would grow up to be like A-Two, a normal girl. Or she could not try, and then she would spend the rest of her life wondering. Or she could try and succeed, and that would mean that she would be different. Always different. Always watching. Always a little afraid.

"Mama," Rosemary whispered.

"With the blood comes choice," Althea had told her. "Only you can choose."

Rosemary looked down at her hands. They trembled, but within them the chrysalis lay still. The chrysalis didn't fear witches or hate them. It knew nothing about good and evil. It knew nothing about life at all. It wasn't meant to know; it was meant to be. It was meant to fly.

"You have to be what you have to be," Rosemary decided. She clasped her hands; she closed her eyes. She tried to think chrysalis thoughts: darkness, tightness, a memory of wind. Nothing happened. She relaxed her face, her fingers. *Please*, she said, but not with her voice, only with her mind, *be beautiful. Be strong.*

A wriggle. A thrust. A tiny crack. And the butterfly emerged from its cocoon, its wings still furled.

Rosemary held her hands flat so that the butterfly would have a platform on which to spread its wings. She watched as the sun dried those wings, making them beautiful and strong. The butterfly hopped, floated toward the ground, made an attempt to meet the air, was blown backward, and then, with guided instinct, rose into the sunlight and flew south.

"Go!" said Rosemary.

She watched until the butterfly was a dot in the sky, until it was gone. Then she examined her hands, front and back. Her own hands, Rosemary's hands; the same hands, but now different. She was now like the others. She was now like the people she loved the most: Althea, Constance, Maria.

From the very depths of Rosemary's soul, a smile began. "Me too," she said. "Me too."

ABOUT THE AUTHOR

Frances M. Wood attended Brown University, then transferred to Stanford University, where she received her bachelor's degree. She also holds a master's degree in library science from the University of California at Berkeley. She lives in North Carolina with her husband, Brian, and their dog, Zephyr. *Becoming Rosemary* is her first novel.